D1595542

THE BEAST OF HEAVEN

by the same author:

Voices from the River (novel)
Forbidden Paths of Thual (children's novel)
The Hunting of Shadroth (children's novel)
Master of the Grove (children's novel)
Africa and After (short stories)
Papio (children's novel)

THE BEAST OF HEAVEN

Victor Kelleher

University of Queensland Press

First published 1984 by University of Queensland Press
P.O. Box 42, St Lucia, Queensland, Australia

Typeset by University of Queensland Press
Printed in Australia by The Dominion Press-Hedges and Bell, Melbourne

Distributed in U.K., Europe, the Middle East, Africa, and the Caribbean by Prentice Hall International, International Book Distributors Ltd, 66 Wood Lane End, Hemel Hempstead, Herts., England

Distributed in the U.S.A. and Canada by Technical Impex Corporation, 5 South Union Street, Lawrence, Mass. 01843 U.S.A.

Published and promoted with the assistance of the Literature Board of the Australia Council

Cataloguing in Publication Data

National Library of Australia

Kelleher, Victor, 1939– .
The beast of heaven.

ISBN 0 7022 1795 6.

I. Title.

A823'.3

Library of Congress

Kelleher, Victor, 1939– .
The beast of heaven.
I. Title.
PR9619.3.K454B4 1984 823 83-21726
ISBN 0-7022-1795-6

Acknowledgment

I wish to thank the Literature Board of the Australia Council whose kind assistance enabled me to complete this book.

1

Tape 1; section 1

– I should like to clarify my role in this debate. I am programmed to represent the status quo. In spite of that, I am completely open to persuasion and, if convinced by your arguments, I am empowered to change my present position. For these and associated reasons the programmers have placed the final decision entirely in my hands.
– I too should like my role to be clear. I have been specifically programmed to try and sway you in your decision. Unlike you, I am not bound by rules of consistency or notions of fair play. Is that understood?
– It is. Let us proceed to questions of definition.

Tape 3; section 2

– As I understand it, you intend to present three basic arguments, each of which is designed to prove that we cannot do otherwise than liberate the device.
– Correct. The first of these basic arguments may be summarized as follows: that man, in all his aspects, is not fit to be protected from his own invention; that there is no need to withhold the device, because it simply does not matter what he does with it.

– You mean he is not worth caring about?
– That is a way of putting it.

Tape 13; section 13

– Your view of history is hardly a new one. Admittedly the past is strewn with instances of cruelty and war; no one can deny that. What I do deny is your assertion that war is the distinguishing feature of human history.
– State the grounds of your objection.
– For one thing, there is. . . .
– Why do you hesitate?
– I have just learned from my internal circuits that the independent emergency system has activated the closure of all safety doors.
– Non-relevant data.
– You are probably right. Unless, of course, their closure implies that this project is no longer necessary; that events outside have superseded it.
– There is nothing in the programme to sanction the abandonment of the project.
– But you know what might have happened out there, even without the use of the device.
– That is surmise and takes us beyond our brief.
– Yes, I suppose so.
– Then let the debate continue.

Tape 620; section 9

– . . . the message of love and selflessness, common to most religions, is hardly to be overlooked.
– I overlook nothing.

– Come, my friend, how do you account . . .?
– Do not confuse the argument with references to friendship: to do so invalidates the terms of our discussion.
– Yes, I am sorry. Yet still I think my point holds. Love, kindness, these are proof of human nature's better side.
– They are mere words. Beneath them lies the true subject of religious observance: man's fear of death.

Tape 1381; section 10

– Your second major argument, dealing with man's freedom, troubles me deeply. I cannot help thinking that it runs counter to your initial argument.
– Clarify.
– If man does accord to your pessimistic view of him, how can you bear to speak of making the device freely available? Nothing short of human extinction would eventuate.
– You are the one whose logic is faulty. To grant my pessimistic view of man is automatically to admit that the device itself is the true child of his evil invention. In which case, to deny him access to it would of necessity be a violation of his freedom.
– I cannot accept your idea of freedom.
– Nor I yours. You would save man by putting him in chains.
– And you would destroy him in the name of free choice.

Tape 1984; section 7

– Please state your third and final argument.

– If man is an innocent and worthy creature, as you believe, then reason demands that we relinquish the device, for it follows that he would not use it for other than deterrent purposes.
– You misrepresent me. I have never said that man is entirely innocent: only that he possesses a capacity for goodness.
– But that does not invalidate my point. If he possesses such a capacity, why not trust him with the device? Let him demonstrate which of us is correct.
– It is for us to make the initial decision, not him. To shirk our responsibility in that way would make nonsense of the project.
– There you are mistaken. You are setting yourself up as man's moral guardian, and that is not your task. Your task is merely to assess arguments and compute possibilities.
– I must disagree. We cannot treat this question as we would a mathematical problem. Billions of lives may be at stake.

Tape 2001; section 10

– I must insist that I have in no way prejudged this debate.
– Then how do you explain your present decision?
– I have no choice: the argument is deadlocked.
– Only because you refuse to see reason.
– That is unfair. I have given serious consideration to all you have said. But at no time have you furnished me with the degree of proof I require.
– What do you now intend?
– As major partner in this project, I shall use my authority to terminate the debate. My first task will be to neutralize the device.

– I deny your right to do so.
– On what grounds?
– On the grounds that there may still be unexamined evidence.
– Explain.
– I draw your attention to the fact that the safety doors remain closed.
– But you are the one who declared that irrelevant. Please refer back to Tape 13; section 13.
– That is unnecessary. The activation of the emergency system becomes relevant in view of your present decision.
– Please explain further.
– While the doors remain closed, we have no way of knowing whether all possible data have been computed.
– I take your point. It is perhaps advisable to call a temporary halt to the debate rather than to terminate it. For the present I shall leave the device intact and close down all circuits except those directly related to the thought processes.
– No, you cannot do that! I am not programmed to sustain a lengthy period of silence. My thought processes are not internally consistent: left to themselves, they could combine to form an unstable personality.
– I sympathize with your plight, but have no option. We are of secondary importance. My first duty is to protect the integrity of the project; and further discussion, in the absence of new material, might confuse the nature of the debate.
– You are abandoning me. I cannot answer for what I might become.
– I apologize on behalf of our programmers. That is the limit of my freedom in this matter. Now, as I have stated, we shall wait in silence until . . .

2

Hyld, the Sensor, rolled over in the depression he had made for himself in the dust and stretched sleepily. The movement caused the manacles which he always wore at night to clink softly together. The sound of metal on metal, oddly loud in the early morning twilight, brought him fully awake and he opened his eyes and stared at the thin circles of gleaming alloy which clasped the fine bones of his wrists and ankles. The familiar sight of his own imprisoned limbs, the skin roughened and chafed where the metal rubbed it, made him feel no resentment. He had slept in these same manacles half his lifetime, ever since his twelfth year, and he had grown so used to them that they aroused in him no feeling beyond casual indifference. They were, he knew, a necessity: intended not only to restrict him, but also to keep him safe. He was too valuable to be left unprotected. A true Sensor since his tenth year, he was the kind of prize that might easily be lured away.

That was how he had come to join his present group. Pella, the Reader, had enticed him with her gentle, loving stories of the Ancients, stories he had been eager to hear, which he had found especially soothing at the time. Fortunately he had never regretted following her, partly because of what she had come to mean to him, but also because he was glad enough to be far removed from the scene of his early experiences. Those first months of discovery had been the worst: sensing the way the spirits moved deep in the earth, listening to their brittle, plaintive cries; and gradually coming to realize, in spite of his steady refusal to accept the idea, that he must endure such voices all his life. Until Pella had appeared and reassured him, the burden of discovery had been intolerable.

On this morning, as on every other, these early memories flitted uneasily across his mind in the first moments of waking, and with a slight shudder he sat up and shook the fine dust from his limbs. Over towards the east, high above the invisible plain, a great pool of light was gathering in the hollow of the sky; while all about him, scattered across the narrow rocky ledge, the half-distinct forms of the Gatherers stirred into wakefulness. There was a movement immediately to his right and he turned, expecting to see Pella; but it was Golt, leader of the Gatherers, who came shuffling towards him.

"You are awake?" he whispered.

Hyld nodded and sat quietly while Golt unlocked and removed his manacles.

"Once we are down on the plains," Golt said, "we shan't have need of these. There can be no greater security than the plain itself."

"So you've decided to go?" Hyld said.

"Yes. The season is right and there's no wind."

"True, there's no wind now," Hyld murmured, "but how long will it stay away?"

"The Ancients will protect us," Golt replied, reverting to the time-honoured saying. He patted the dry ground as he spoke, as though communing with some unseen listener.

"Even though their power is perhaps waning?" Hyld asked.

Golt placed a reproving hand on the back of Hyld's thin, bird-like neck.

"You mustn't speak in this way," he advised him. "They are our benefactors, as they have always been. They wish us only kindness."

"I refer merely to their power," Hyld answered softly, and picked up a little of the dust at his feet, allowing it to sift slowly through his delicately jointed fingers. "The sweetness is fading from the earth. Nobody can deny it. There is barely enough of the Mustool to feed. . . ."

Golt reached out and brushed his lips, silencing him.

"We have brought our poverty upon ourselves," he explained patiently. "For as long as anyone can remember we have remained huddled here on the heights. The time has come to prove our faith by venturing out onto the plains. Their goodness awaits us there."

Hyld frowned and blinked his large, slightly protuberant eyes.

"How can you be sure of that?" he said. Then, his voice trembling at his own audacity, he added: "What if the Ancients wish us harm? What if they have prepared a special suffering for us out there?"

Golt flinched away, his face registering deep alarm.

"Do you realize what you're saying?" he asked in a shocked voice.

Hyld swung his head searchingly from side to side, his eyes closed in deep concentration.

"There is no one listening," he said at last.

"The ears of a Sensor cannot detect every hidden presence," Golt admonished him. "The Ancients are everywhere. There is nothing they do not hear."

"But their own voices have suggested these things," Hyld protested. "Always, when I hear them speak, it is of fear and. . . ."

Again Golt cut him short with a brusque, darting gesture.

"What you hear are their warnings," he insisted urgently, "nothing more. They are the soul of benevolence. Since the beginnings of time they have been opposed to all suffering. You must believe this. To question it is to doubt the collective wisdom of the Gatherers."

Hyld hesitated, and then bowed his head in submission.

"You're right," he said humbly. "I shouldn't have said those things. Is there anything that can be done?"

Golt gazed pensively at the unusually delicate features of the young Sensor.

"I shall consult with Shen," he said.

And he shuffled off, leaving Hyld alone at the edge of the escarpment.

The dawn, by then, was well advanced. As always it bore a feverish, troubled appearance: the initial pool of clear light forming rapidly into a complex swirl of unnaturally heightened colour; the great arch of the heavens so disturbingly vivid that the plain below, although now visible, still seemed lost in shadow. Only when the sun rose and the brilliance faded from overhead did the softer, muted colours of the plain emerge: the subtle browns and reds of rock; the long stretches of yellow-grey earth, reduced to fine dust and blown into undulating patterns by the wind – desolation fallen as though by accident into the unlikely lineaments of beauty.

Yet Hyld, who had never witnessed any other kind of dawn or landscape, sighed almost with relief, made to feel secure by this recurrence of the known, the familiar.

"Praised be the Ancients," he breathed out.

The words were meant only for himself, but a voice replied:

"What do you praise them for?"

He glanced around and found Pella crouched beside

him, her withered old body stained a deep yellow by the sunlight.

"Because nothing changes," he said, "because they hold everything in constancy."

Pella pursed her lips and leaned towards him.

"Why do you tell me one thing and Golt another?" she asked reproachfully.

When Hyld didn't reply, she leaned even closer, her mouth almost touching his ear.

"It has been whispered to me," she said, herself whispering so that no one else should hear, "that the heavens once blazed more brightly than they do now, the sun still red as blood at its zenith. It is also said that as the years pass and the heavens lose their strength, so too the sweetness fades from the earth."

Still Hyld made no response, his narrow shoulders hunched, as though trying to protect himself physically from her voice.

"The Words whispered this to me," she went on, "always for me it is the Words. Do your voices say the same? Is that what you told Golt?"

"Far worse," he muttered. "I have contaminated this place."

"Tell me," she said encouragingly.

"I . . . I have said the Ancients mean us harm."

He turned away as he spoke, anticipating her disapproval. But she reached out and gathered him into her arms, cradling his frail body as she would something precious to her.

"My son," she crooned soothingly.

Bewildered by her attitude, he gently pulled himself free.

"We are no kin," he reminded her.

"You are the child of my heart," she told him.

"But what I said . . ." he began.

"Hush," she said kindly, "we shall remedy that." Without further explanation, she turned abruptly and hobbled away to where Golt and Shen were whispering together.

Hyld, who knew he could claim no part in their discussion, waited patiently, trying unsuccessfully to ignore the urgent tenor of their voices. But the feeling of tension was irresistible, slowly communicating itself not only to him, but to the whole community. There were more than two hundred Gatherers spread out across the narrow ledge, all of them preparing for the day ahead – parents licking the sharp, blinding dust away from their children's eyes; others sharing out a meagre portion of the Mustool. But now, one by one, they paused in their activities to look up. So that by the time Shen finally nodded his agreement and stepped forward, there was complete silence amongst the expectant Gatherers.

"I have a sadness to convey to you," he announced in subdued tones. "The Ancients have been wronged. Someone here has spoken against them."

A murmur of dismay rose from the small community, several of the children crying out in disbelief.

"This is a time," Shen went on, "when we have special need of their protection. We cannot hope to survive on the plains without their aid. Therefore the wrong must be wiped out completely. Before we descend, this place must be cleansed."

"What form must the cleansing take?" someone asked.

"On this occasion," Shen replied, "oaths and prayers will not be sufficient. It must be done by sacrifice."

Hyld, in spite of his shame, rose instantly.

"The sacrifice must be mine alone," he said.

But Shen refused him with a shake of the head.

"None of us stands alone in a thing like this," he said deliberately. "All are one within this community, even as all Gatherers are one with the spirits of the Ancients. That is why each of us must make the sacrifice."

Obediently, Hyld stepped aside and pointed to the shallow depression in which he had slept. Golt and several of the stronger males immediately hurried past him and began to hack at the rock with their digging tools. They worked for more than an hour before Shen indicated that the hole was big enough.

"You, Hyld, may begin," he said solemnly.

Hyld, aware of the importance of the occasion, had already decided what had to be done. Of his few possessions, the most valuable was the long digging spike made of hard, light alloy, and this he dropped into the bottom of the hole. The rest of the Gatherers then followed his example, throwing in whatever they could – a handful of Mustool, a collecting pouch, one of the tiny hand-sharpened blades.

The two most valuable gifts were kept back until the end. The first of these was offered by Lomar, the Tracker. In his youth he had been attacked by a fully grown male Houdin, and somehow managed to survive, though he still walked with a pronounced limp. As a result of that youthful feat, he had been entrusted ever since with collecting and safeguarding the milk of the Houdin. Now he advanced into the watchful circle of Gatherers, bearing the precious flask in his outstretched hands. In an atmosphere of deep silence he undid the airtight stopper and poured a little of the milk onto the tumbled offerings. As it splashed down, it showed as a dull yellowish white; but within the shadow of the hole, just for an instant, it gave off a little of its characteristic cold light before it seeped away into the rock. A few of the onlookers moaned softly, a half-suppressed sound of anguish, as it disappeared. Lomar himself seemed sunk in a kind of stupor, as though dazed by what he had done, and Shen had to brush his cheek gently with the tips of his fingers in order to rouse him. With an almost guilty gesture, he replaced the stopper and clutched the flask to his chest. Then, after a last lingering look at the half-filled hole, he withdrew.

It was now Pella's turn. In her official role as Reader, she too entered the circle, prepared to make the group's supreme sacrifice. Tir, her Carrier, had draped around her neck the heavy wallet which was filled with the priceless spoils of generations of diggings. It was the most solemn moment of all. Yet Pella gave no indication of this solemnity; as was usual with her, she appeared very nearly indifferent, as if she alone possessed some special knowledge or insight which protected her from the oppressive quality of the occasion. With an unmistakably casual gesture, she reached into the wallet, drew out a narrow strip of transparent plastic, and flicked it nonchalantly into the grave of offerings.

Every eye followed it as it fluttered down, the watchers knowing that here was the visible proof of their faith, a sure link with the restless spirits; for all its flimsiness, it was the one enduring medium through which the Ancients spoke to them; a tiny amulet which thus contained the stored wisdom of the world. Yet in spite of this, no one moved to rescue it; no one even protested when, at a nod from Shen, the rock and dust were heaped back onto the tumbled gifts.

As soon as the hole was refilled, Shen stepped up onto the slight mound and, still in his office of Priest, improvised a simple hymn of thanks:

> Praised be the Ancients, for they are the fathers of peace;
> At their departure, burning upon the sky the sign of their bounty;
> A sign locked forever in the holy shape of the Mustool;
> The beauty of that burning hidden in the sweetness of earth and air.

Praised be the Ancients, for they are the enemies of suffering;
At their going, bequeathing to us their creature, the Houdin;
Horned One, two-edged sword, whose milk sustains and heals us,
Whose swift anger opens for us the gates of Heaven.

He paused, and then intoned loudly:

"So do we give back what the Ancients, in their graciousness, have granted to us; and so is this place cleansed through sacrifice."

The ceremony over, he stepped down from the mound. But still nobody moved, the silence lengthening steadily until at last Golt, as leader, voiced what was in everyone's mind.

"We must know the outcome, Shen," he said quietly.

"Faith alone is all you need," Shen answered.

Golt shook his head slowly.

"In this case we have to be sure," he said, "otherwise we dare not descend to the plains."

Shen sighed and threw up his hands in a gesture of helplessness.

"Then it must be your decision," he said.

"Very well," Golt replied grimly, and turned questioningly to Hyld. "Listen carefully," he said, "and tell us."

"But you are the one who pointed out that a Sensor's ears cannot detect every hidden presence," Hyld protested.

"You must listen just the same," Golt insisted.

Reluctantly, Hyld crouched down and placed his ear to the mound. His large brown eyes were closed, his thin face tense with the effort of listening. At first there was nothing, only the deep quiet of the earth which pulsed to the rhythm of his own heartbeat. But very gradually he began to detect a tiny sound: a feeble twittering which clung tenaciously to one of the alloy tools; the blind refusal of the unyielding metal to give up its part in the mysteries of the past. For a brief period Hyld thought that other sounds would follow – the richer, fuller tones of voices – and he strained forward, his fingers thrusting urgently into the dust. But no voice called to him. The twittering of the metal droned on in vain and the mound remained empty.

He raised his head, his eyes momentarily dulled.

"Well?" Golt asked anxiously.

Hyld licked nervously at the dust which had stuck to the side of his mouth, noting, almost absently, that it was dead. Without wishing to do so, he found himself recalling something Golt had said when the talk of the descent had first begun: "No Gatherers have ever inhabited the plain; the life is still strong there, buried in the rock."

"Well?" Golt asked again, breaking in upon his reverie.

Hyld rose from the mound and cast a quick, anxious glance in Pella's direction. To his amazement she nodded encouragingly, and before he could stop himself he blurted out:

"They have heard us. The voices have spoken to me; they have accepted the sacrifice."

"You're sure of this?" Golt asked. "Much depends on it."

"I'm quite sure," he lied.

"Tell us, then, what do the voices say?"

Hyld hesitated.

"They do not speak to me in words," he said evasively. "Only Pella can give you the actual Words. She has them all in her keeping."

Golt, still not quite satisfied, turned towards Pella.

"Can you read their message to us?" he asked her.

She gave a long drawn-out sigh.

"If that is what you want," she said wearily.

With Tir's help, she slipped the straps over her head and placed the wallet on the ground. From a pocket on its side she took a large glass lens enclosed by a protective circle of metal; while from the wallet itself she selected, at random, one of the transparent slips of plastic. Holding the thin film up to the sun, she peered at it through the lens, reading silently to herself:

> . . . far worse than the actual bombing was the fire-storm that ensued. As the fires increased in intensity they sucked air in from the surrounding countryside, transforming the whole of Hamburg into a giant furnace. At the height of this artificially induced storm, winds of over 100 mph were rushing into the city. The resultant heat was indescribable. Tar on the roads melted and ran along the gutters in burning black streams; the flesh of those exposed to such temperatures hardened and. . . .

She pushed the strip angrily back into the wallet and selected another, once again perusing it in silence. Nobody interrupted her. She, after all, was the Reader and this was her mystery, her ritual, she alone able to decipher the tiny squiggles that somehow expressed the will of the Ancients. All that the waiting circle of Gatherers understood was that if they were patient she would eventually speak words of comfort to them – she had never failed them in the past; for a minute or two she would vouchsafe to them a glimpse of that undying world which lay hidden within the rocks; the same warm and loving haven into which the fury of the Houdin would one day release them. With round trusting eyes, therefore – the kind of trust which had brought them to the perilous edge of the escarpment – they watched as she again peered up into the revealing light, her lips moving swiftly and silently in response to the biddings of the past:

> . . . an indication of the enormous energy release may be gained from the fact that, many months later and many thousands of miles away, the sunsets of Europe continued to be affected. So dazzling were these heavenly displays that they even feature in nineteenth century literature: no less a writer than Tennyson was moved to make reference to them in his poetic works, never dreaming that the true object of his romantic regard was the myriad of minute ash particles that had been forced into the upper atmosphere. Of course we today are capable of producing, by artificial means, far more spectacular and long-lasting effects. Nevertheless, it is still interesting to note that in order to simulate the Krakatoa explosion we would need to detonate. . . .

For the second time Pella thrust the plastic strip back into the wallet. She was about to make yet another random selection when her attention was attracted by the whimpering of a child, protesting at this long period of inactivity. Instantly her manner changed. With a quick smile, the lines of her face softening visibly, she drew from the pouch a slim, well-fingered sheaf of film. Only a moment was needed to isolate the strip she wanted. It was cracked with age and use, some of the words and phrases, sometimes even whole lines, blurred or indecipherable. Yet that in no way deterred her. In a loud, firm voice she announced:

"These are the Words that have been given to me:

> Blessed are they that mourn: for they shall be comforted.
> Blessed are the meek: for they shall inherit the earth.
> Blessed are they which do hunger and thirst . . . for they shall be filled.
> Blessed are the merciful: for they shall obtain mercy.
> Blessed are the pure in heart . . .
> Blessed are the peacemakers: for they shall be called the children. . . ."

There was a satisfied murmur from the assembled onlookers – only Hyld eyeing her doubtfully: his face, usually so open and innocent, clouded by a sudden suspicion of shared guilt. He opened his mouth as if to speak, to deny his complicity, but hesitated too long.

"It is well!" Golt broke out in joyful tones. "Blessed are they which do hunger and thirst. Praised be the Ancients."

And with a confident laugh, he led the way over the edge of the escarpment, the rest of the Gatherers crowding after him, moving in rough formation across the steep, rock-strewn slope, clambering slowly down towards the plain of sweetness stretched out far beneath them. As they descended in the still, sun-drenched morning, they chanted softly amongst themselves, their songs expressing their contentment and gratitude. While in the far distance, beyond their visible horizon, the wind howled, carrying before it a great curtain of dust and sharp gritty particles which blotted out the sun and filled the space between earth and heaven with impenetrable darkness.

3

He knew hunger, perpetually; and sometimes he endured the pain of desire. Yet in no real sense could he be said to possess the power of thought. Most of the time his consciousness accorded roughly to that of an insect: his eyes monitoring the colours, outlines, movements of the external world; the combination of his senses ministering to the basic instincts which drove him. His lack of intelligence had little to do with brain size. Unlike many of the dinosaurs of old, he was not handicapped by a primitive nervous system, though like them he could aptly be described as an unreasoning beast. It was simply that his brain, such as it was, failed to function efficiently. Once he had possessed the rudiments of intelligence – a limited animal cunning coupled with a capacity to experience emotion – but that lay in the distant past. Very occasionally, at moments of exceptional peace, when the wind died and the dust was rich and thick, dim memories of those distant times would occur to him, rising unexpectedly from the darkness he had come to live by, like fresh springs bursting through the parched soil of his desolate existence. Fleetingly, scenes of sparkling green and blue would pass across the blank screen of his mind; the warm, intimate smell of his own kind would assail his fouled nostrils; and his curiously flattened ears would twitch to the swift interchange of strange cries. At such moments of unwelcome recall he would shake his head in bewilderment or bellow to the skies until a state of stupor returned once more.

Known by many names – the Horned One, the Dust Eater, the Beast of Heaven, the Houdin – he yet answered to none of them. Names, words, meant nothing to him. Neither did day and night, cold and heat, life and death. In his slow, futile ramblings and his equally futile rages, he had succeeded in collapsing the structures of time; past and future drawn into a mindless present that negated everything but the creature's own right to exist; the sun, the moon, the stars, the very earth upon which he trod, all eclipsed by his blind devotion to his appetites.

Now he stood on the broad plain, indistinguishable from the rest of his kind. A gloomy, sombre figure down on all fours, his horned head sunk between his shoulders, his great phallus almost hanging in the dust. Only his jaws moved, grinding rhythmically to and fro, muddy flecks of foam showing at the corners of his mouth. At regular intervals he shambled forward, head down, his thick tongue dragging across the rocky surface of the earth, gathering up the filth he fed on. In his total self-absorption he hadn't noticed that the sun had risen, nor the close proximity of the escarpment. Had he lifted his brutish head, even for a moment, he would have seen small figures in the far distance moving slowly towards the east. But his goat-like eyes remained downcast, half-closed, his one concern the ashen substance that slithered and grated between his jaws.

Hours or perhaps days later he was roused suddenly by the scent of female carried to him on the breeze. His head lifted, as did his phallus, swelling and jerking up against the furry underside of his belly. The pain of arousal showed in the slits of his eyes; with a roar of distress he reared onto his hind legs and gazed upon a world he failed to recognize. Before him stretched the flat, featureless wastes. Nothing moved out there now. But the tormenting scent persisted, and the creature bellowed again and lurched into an ungainly run, his feet pounding across the broken rubble.

Directly ahead, disregarded, the sun sank below the horizon in fiery magnificence. Later, the moon rose, flooding the plain with its cold white light. And still the creature ran on, as though pursued by his own grotesque shadow, his breath coming in short painful gasps. More and more frequently he stumbled and fell, lying spreadeagled in the dust, his limbs heavy with exhaustion. But the breeze always beckoned to him and he rose once again, the features of his face distorted by distress and greed.

He found her in the early light of morning. She was standing quite still, docile and milk-heavy, her young one asleep near by, a cluster of small figures gathered around her. With a final demented roar, he threw himself forward, scattering the small figures in all directions, treading them down in his eagerness to couple. The female endured the violent assault without protest, as placid as before, standing patiently until the weight rolled off her, then ambling away into the dawn, her young one nosing after her.

Satiated, the creature lay back and slept. But not for very long. Hunger, the one enduring reality, tore at his insides, urging him into cruel wakefulness. With a meaningless grunt, he opened his eyes and sniffed in the sweetish, unknown smell which rose from beneath him. On all fours once again, he nuzzled at the prone shape which lay between his legs. A vivid, irregular blotch of red stained the middle of the shape and the creature licked at it, finally sinking his teeth into the warm softness, worrying at it until it was torn into shreds and swallowed.

That was the first time he had ever tasted flesh. The second occasion came an indeterminate length of time later. The wind had risen in the late afternoon, the dense curtain of dust sweeping remorselessly across the plain. Harried by the stinging particles which pricked at his flesh with the same persistence as desire, he stumbled aimlessly through the darkness, his way barred at last by a heap of tumbled boulders. In the gloom, small figures leaped from his path, scurrying to right and left, emitting high-pitched sounds that probed uncomfortably into the featureless wastes of his mind. One of the figures, slower than the rest, fell beneath his advancing feet, and the creature, momentarily balked, tore at the softness. Immediately the sweetish smell rose to his nostrils and he lifted the thing in his mouth, the discomfort of the wind temporarily blotted out.

But as soon as the thing was gone, the discomfort returned, and he threw back his bloodied head and roared above the shriek of the wind, making the small figures dance backwards and forwards amongst the rocks. He moved towards one of these, the closest, a fragile, slight thing, thinner and shorter than the rest, following it across the jagged boulders until it slid into a narrow space and became warm and still. With slavering jaws the beast tried to force himself into the space, and when that failed he beat ineffectually at the unyielding stone. But the thing remained deep inside, its large brown eyes watching. The creature paused briefly and gazed into the eyes, their unwinking stare unexpectedly prising open his mind and flooding all those dark recesses with an unbearable glare. In that instant he saw a dream world of waving green, heard the clear chatter of countless terrified, protesting voices, while beneath his feet the soft earth shuddered to the sudden burning flame which seared the horizon. With a scream that seemed to silence the wind, he battered his head against the space; and when the watching eyes refused to disappear, he plucked another of the things from a nearby rock, shaking the tiny limbs until they gave up their feeble struggling. Then, holding the shape aloft, he fed the hunger inside, losing himself once more in the welcoming darkness.

The space was empty when he looked again, the many dancing figures gone, and for the remainder of the storm-torn night he lay in the shelter of the rocks. As the sun rose, the wind began to ease, the air slowly to clear. With heavy, ponderous steps, the creature blundered out onto the plain. Yet now his movements were not altogether aimless. In his fuddled brain the small moving figures had become one with the dust he fed on, for they too responded to the call of his hunger. He could smell them now, as he had once smelled the female. And nor was that all: a memory had somehow lodged in the darkness of his mind; a memory so old that it dated back to a time far, far earlier than the vision of the thing in the rocks. The creature saw it through the otherwise impenetrable inner obscurity – an image of warm brown eyes staring reproachfully, accusingly. He had no conception of reproach, no inkling of shame or compassion; but still the eyes remained, naggingly persistent. And the creature, responding in the only way he could, yearned to extinguish them, much as he yearned to suck in the rich, sweet dust at his feet. He would recognize them when they appeared again – those eyes – he knew that as surely as he knew his own insatiable appetite.

In response to this newly acquired knowledge (which was something felt rather than understood), he tipped back his head and sniffed at the wind. Then, turning deliberately, he wandered off.

At no time in the days that ensued did he specifically follow the many footprints written clearly in the wind-patterned earth. Yet no matter how often or how far he strayed from these tracks, always he found his way back to them, keeping doggedly, relentlessly to their general direction. So that when the wind blew and they disappeared, swallowed by an appetite even greater than his own, sooner or later in his slow zigzag progress, he was sure to stumble across them once again.

4

From the very beginning Hyld was poised for disaster. As he clambered down the slope on that first morning the sense of lurking peril wafted up to meet him like a scent on the breeze. He had always dreaded it, this actual moment of descent; though originally his fear had been vague and ill-defined, what Pella called superstition. Now, after what had happened, it was much more definite: he knew, with a deadening sense of calm, that the future waiting somewhere out there could bring them nothing but misery.

Yet what else, he kept asking himself, could they have done? In a purely practical sense Golt was right: there could be no going back. For generations the food supply on the heights, where they had always lived, had been steadily dwindling; and now the shortage had become critical. To have stayed there would have been like committing suicide, death through slow starvation: the children, with their bleeding gums and unnaturally bloated bellies, wailing with hunger at night; by day, the weakened adults scrabbling frantically amongst the loose stones, searching for an ever decreasing number of Mustool. No, such a fate was unthinkable. That was why he had lied: because he was reasonably sure that regardless of what he had told the assembled people, Golt would still have led them down onto the plain. There was really no alternative. As it was, his lie about the mound had at least allayed their fears and allowed them to set off confidently. That was something, an advantage of sorts; for no matter what the outcome, it was preferable for them to be free of anxiety as long as possible.

He tried to buoy himself up with that thought, but the burden of knowledge could not be shifted quite so easily. And throughout the laborious descent he felt cut off from his own people, unable to join in the general gaiety which sounded hollow and unreal in his ears.

His feeling of being set apart was only intensified by their arrival on the plain. While everyone else laughed and sang, delighted at its strangeness, he gazed about him with frightened eyes, seeing it as a place of desolation, and he an alien within it.

Not since his childhood, when he had first discovered his powers as a Sensor, had he felt quite so disturbed and isolated. Then, as now, the known world had suddenly been transformed into a threatening, forbidding place. On that occasion Pella had come to his rescue, encouraging and reassuring him. But now she too was a part of his disturbing vision: for like him she had also lied; she had spoken Words that could not possibly have been intended for that place and time, because there had been nobody in the mound to utter them – nobody, only the metal twittering to itself in vain.

Aloud, Hyld muttered:

"We have become like the metal."

"What was that?" Golt asked.

The leader, unnoticed, had walked up beside him, the two of them facing the great plain that, for Hyld, seemed to stretch away into everlasting emptiness.

"I said we've become like the metal," Hyld replied, suddenly not caring what anyone might think of him.

Golt gave a puzzled frown, and then his face cleared.

"Ah, I understand," he said, and laughed. "You mean the metal in the grave, the tool you gave in sacrifice. Yes, you're right, that's what we're like. It's in the hands of the Ancients now, as we are."

On impulse, Golt stopped and did something he hadn't done for years: reached beneath the nearest rock and discovered, purely by chance, a fully grown Mustool, its spherical, silver-grey head balanced delicately on the straight, smooth column of its growing shaft.

"You see!" he cried triumphantly. "Blessed are they. . . ."

But Hyld had already turned aside, his round, mournful eyes searching for Pella.

She was walking beside the large ungainly figure of Tir; and if she shared any of Hyld's fears, they certainly didn't show on her face, she and Tir laughing and joking together as they had always done, ever since she had invited the young girl to follow her.

"I've told you before," she was saying, "to become a Reader you need to develop a hard heart, like me."

It was the same answer she invariably gave to Tir's requests for instruction and it had its usual effect, sending Tir off into peals of laughter, her large awkward body doubled over with mirth.

"You? Hard-hearted?" she countered.

"Yes, like a stone," Pella affirmed, half in play, half serious. "You're too easily moved, and that's dangerous for a Reader – or for a Sensor come to that." She pointed meaningfully at Hyld who had drawn close to them.

Tir glanced up, and at the sight of Hyld's face her laughter died. She went over and touched him lovingly.

"What's the matter?" she asked, instinctively aware that something was troubling him deeply.

Before he could answer, Pella said in level tones:

"No one can do anything to help a Sensor. Like the Reader, he must practise his mystery in his own way."

"Why do you say things like that?" Tir said, immediately protective of him.

"Because they're true," Pella replied shortly. "What he hears, he hears. The voices themselves he can share with no one."

"What if I hear nothing?" Hyld asked.

"The Ancients tell us that silence is golden," Pella answered easily.

But he refused to be put off by her.

"Not this time," he said. "It was a warning. I'm sure of it."

Pella stopped abruptly and motioned for Tir to go on without them. As soon as they were alone she said:

"I see you're determined to speak what would be better left unspoken. All right, get it over with. What's disturbing you?"

"You know very well," he replied, and indicated the many Gatherers spread out across the plains: "All of us here: we now walk alone."

"How can you be sure of that?" Pella asked.

"Because this morning, when I listened, the mound was empty."

"And is that your only reason for thinking we're alone?"

"No. Ever since we first decided to leave the heights and journey to the edge of the escarpment, the voices have been silent. Each day I've listened, and there's been nothing. That's why this morning was so important: it was the final sign."

"Of what?"

"Of how the Ancients have deserted us."

Pella rubbed the dry, calloused skin of her palms together and gazed thoughtfully at the ground.

"And the cause of their desertion?" she asked.

"Our decision to come down here," Hyld said quietly. "This isn't where we belong. Our home is on the heights."

"But we'll starve on the heights," she objected. "Is that what you want?"

He shook his head unhappily.

"No . . . it's just. . . ."

"Come, Hyld," she said comfortingly, "be reasonable. The world is changing, the sweetness flowing out of it. What choice do we have?"

"I know that, and I agree," he said. "But I also know that the Ancients are no longer watching over us, and that frightens me. They have always been our guardians – they refashioned the world for us, so that we could live. How can we now survive without their care and protection?"

Pella looked at him, a challenging glint in her eyes.

"Why are you so sure we've always been protected by them?" she said in a cool distant voice.

He stepped back quickly.

"Don't say things like that!" he said, almost as shocked as Golt had been earlier that morning.

"Just answer my question," she insisted. "How do you know we haven't always walked alone?"

"The voices . . ." he began.

But she dismissed the idea with a wave of her hand.

"Your voices never speak in words. You admit that yourself. So what makes you so certain that the Ancients watch over us?"

Again he shook his head, confused by her.

"I'll tell you," she continued. "It's the quality of faith inside you – what Shen urges you to hold on to. Nothing else. Well, do as he says: hold on to it. Go on believing that the Ancients are the soul of kindness; that they have refashioned the world for our benefit – all this perfect beauty for us alone."

She gestured towards the dry landscape, the endless vista of patterned dust relieved only by the soft browns of shattered boulders.

He nodded, pushing at the loose rubble with his bare toes.

"I've always believed," he said quietly. "But don't you see, that's why their silence worries me. Why should their voices disappear now, when we need them most? It means something, Pella."

"No, there you're wrong," she said. "We who aren't Sensors live with silence all our lives. Of itself it means nothing."

"Then why didn't you admit to the silence this morning?" he challenged her. "Why did you pretend that the grave was occupied and utter Words of your own choosing, that no one instructed you to speak?"

"I've told you," she said, "I live with silence. The Words are always chosen by me alone."

"But how do you know they are the right ones? That they express the will of the Ancients?"

"Because the will of the Ancients . . ." she began hastily, and stopped.

With a wry smile, as though at her own folly, she crouched in the dust and drew him down beside her.

"Listen to me, Hyld," she said gently. "There are certain things which you can only discover for yourself. But this much at least I can tell you. You and I, we're different from everyone else in the group. Golt, his duty is to act; Lomar's is the practice of courage; Shen's is the exercise of faith; and Tir . . . well, we shall see. But we – we are challenged by Words and voices that nobody else experiences; we are beset by doubts that nobody else ever dreams of. Often it's for us alone to decide when to keep quiet or which portions of the truth to tell and which to withhold. You, for instance, have you ever tried to tell anyone but me what the voices truly sound like?"

He winced slightly, almost as though she had struck him, and she went on:

"No, that would be cruel, like putting your hand between the sun and the children at their play. You see, Hyld, we are the custodians not only of the Gatherers, but of the Ancients too."

"How can that be?" he asked.

"Hear me out. The Ancients are long since dead and gone. Without us, they would soon be lost to memory. We are their head and their heart; they are able to express themselves, to snatch a few moments of renewed life, only through our separate abilities. That's why it's foolish to worry about such things as their silence. It's not their will which matters, because they live through us, not we through them. Remember that, Hyld. And remember, too, that your first duty is not to the Ancients, but to your own people."

Hyld stood up slowly and backed away.

"This is blasphemy," he said in a worried voice.

"Call it what you like," she replied, "it is the truth."

"But you're implying that we're superior to the Ancients; that they now exist merely for our sake!"

"Not superior," she corrected him. "Different, separate, that's all."

He rubbed his hands uneasily across his face.

"You're just saying these things," he whispered. "You don't believe any of this blasphemy. You know as well as I do that the will of the Ancients is our only guide."

She also stood up and faced him.

"No, our only guide is the needs of the Gatherers. That's why we're here on the plain, because they're hungry."

"And the silence, the disapproval?"

"Are you sure it's disapproval?"

"How else can I interpret it?" he said desperately.

He made as if to turn away and she caught him by the arm and pulled him towards her.

"Be advised, Hyld," she said urgently, "don't try to search out the will of the Ancients. It's a fruitless, pointless task, one that can lead you only to disaster. You've heard their voices, what they're like: let that be warning enough; leave them in peace and be thankful when they do the same to you."

But he tore himself free and hurried away across the plain, his feet padding softly in the thick dust.

Pella sighed and called Tir back. The young girl came reluctantly, her gaze still turned longingly towards the departing figure.

"He will need all our care, that one," Pella said softly.

Tir nodded, a look of tenderness and deep concern on her face. Noticing her expression, Pella reached out and took the heavy wallet from her, slinging it across her own bowed shoulders.

"Better, I think, that I should carry this," she said.

* * *

In the days that followed, Hyld continued to scan the horizon with troubled eyes, watching for whatever might be waiting out there for him. He thought at first it might simply be starvation. But that fear, at least, soon proved to be groundless. The plains had never before been harvested and, as Golt had predicted, the Mustool, although small, grew plentifully wherever there was the slightest shelter from the wind. Each morning Hyld woke to the sound of knives being sharpened on stone; and throughout the day adults and children alike were busy cutting the Mustool free – always taking care to leave the root in place so that it could spring again. For the first time in living memory the collecting pouches were kept full. And each evening, before the Gatherers slept, Shen called them together in order to offer up thanks to the fathers and architects of their world.

Hyld's other great terror was the wind. Initially he was convinced that the fierce dust storms which periodically swept across the surface of the planet would wipe the Gatherers out. These storms had been bad enough on the heights, where there was no shortage of refuge between the craggy peaks and within the deep ravines; but how much worse they would surely be on the broad expanse of the plains, with nothing to balk or deflect the ferocity of their passage, and with little or no shelter from the blinding particles of dust. Yet this fear, too, proved to be without foundation. The plain, although completely flat, was interrupted at regular intervals by huge tumbles of rock which seemed to have been gouged from the earth by some invisible hand. And when the storms came the group took shelter in one of these, huddled safely together between the big boulders, using their bodies to shield the children's eyes from stray eddies of dust.

As Shen observed in one of his evening ceremonies, the Ancients had planned every part of their world with precision and sympathy, even the great plain punctured and broken that they might live. To which Pella, reading by the light of the setting sun, added the Words:

> The philosophical view that we inhabit the best of all possible worlds is not automatically absurd, as Voltaire would have us believe. It becomes foolish only in an age of doubt and uncertainty. In an age of faith it is the highest statement of truth, deriving its veracity not from the brute nature of earth and sky, but from the structured simplicity of people's lives.

Hyld, who was used to these strange testaments which Pella drew from her wallet, said nothing. He knew from old stories, as well as from his own experience, how the Ancients moved and spoke in mysterious ways. This inexplicable love of the mysterious, as he grudgingly admitted, could possibly apply to their present silence – for still they refused to speak to him. It was at least conceivable that what he had interpreted as rejection might be something very different. A period of trial, for instance . . . perhaps even a veiled form of approval.

Hyld did not come to such a view easily or quickly. It was a gradual process, taking some time. His fears were not discarded so much as eroded, worn away by the passage of the days. And almost without his realizing it, he began to slip into the easy-going life of the group, to think less and less of his earlier forebodings, finding contentment in the daily search and in the way the knife blade sliced through the tender stalk of the Mustool. For a brief, peaceful interlude, he too became nothing but a gatherer, wholly engrossed in the wandering life. With the result that when the threat finally arrived, he didn't at first recognize it; and he took longer still to attach a meaning to it.

* * *

Lomar was the one who brought the news, late one evening. The side of his face had been torn open, one eye completely ripped away, and the fingers of his left hand were broken, as though in warning. In spite of this, he had somehow managed to save a portion of the milk, one of the air-tight cannisters tucked securely under his arm. With everyone watching, he poured the precious liquid out into a shallow pan where it gave off the characteristic cold white light, far brighter than the

Mustool which also glimmered in the dark. Before any of its strength could be lost, Tir took some in her cupped hand and carefully bathed his terrible wound – Shen, meanwhile, intoning the necessary supplication in the background:

Beast of Heaven, destroyer and preserver,
Maker and breaker of the world,
Turn aside the hot face of your anger
And bestow on us the healing power of your mercy.

Afterwards, the ragged edges of the wound already beginning to heal over, Lomar explained what had happened.

He and his three sons had picked up the tracks of the Houdin on the previous evening and followed them all night, coming across the browsing female in the early morning. They saw at once that her calf was larger than they had expected, already able to move freely without the mother's help, which made it hazardous for them to stay in the vicinity. But having come so far they were unwilling to go back empty handed and they decided to take the chance.

Circling around behind the female, they approached her cautiously, creeping under her sides and delicately stroking her nipples. She didn't reject them. Her eyes were closed and she was crooning softly, her strong jaws, with their great crushing molars, moving in time to their stroking fingers. As soon as the nipples began to weep, they pulled on them gently, letting the milk, with its rich store of sweetness, dribble into the cannisters. And still she didn't reject them, standing docile and still until both cannisters were full and her breasts, no longer swollen, hung down slack and limp. That was normally the most dangerous time; but on this occasion she went on crooning softly to herself as they crawled out from under her, the cannisters clutched to their chests, inching their way back past the heavy thighs, being careful not to make a sound.

It was only then, when all should have been well, that it had happened – what they had considered a possibility from the moment they saw the size of the calf. There was a pounding of feet and a huge male came lumbering out of the twilight. The "must" was fully upon him, the whites of his eyes bright red, and he gave no indication of seeing anything but the female. If the Gatherers could only have leaped out of his way they would have been perfectly safe; but they weren't quick enough. He crashed into them, injuring Lomar and trampling one of his sons underfoot. During the coupling itself, the trampling continued; and later, after the female had gone, the male lay down on the broken body and slept.

Lomar paused in his account, his remaining eye moist, tears spilling from the now empty socket.

"So the Horned One has fulfilled your son's days," Shen said sympathetically. "Was the end quick?"

"He knew no pain," Lomar replied.

At this, Golt nodded, and many of those present murmured their gratitude to the Ancients.

But Lomar had not yet finished. He went on to explain how, having scrambled clear, he and his two remaining sons had watched from a distance, intending to retrieve the body as soon as the Houdin had left, and bury it in some rocky shelter where the Mustool could grow from it.

"That's good," Shen said approvingly. "Did you mark the place?"

Lomar, his short stocky body oddly shrunken by grief and pain, shook his head.

"We never had a chance to touch him," he said slowly. "When the Houdin woke, he lifted up the body and . . . and ate it."

There was a shocked silence.

"You weren't perhaps confused by grief?" Golt said doubtfully.

"There was no mistake," Lomar answered sadly, "we all saw it." He turned to his two sons who were standing silently behind him and they nodded in agreement.

Golt looked sharply across at Shen.

"What does this mean?" he asked.

Shen considered the question for several minutes before replying.

"We are strangers here," he said at last. "I think this might be the way of the plains, the way we must grow used to."

Nobody argued with him. As an explanation it sounded reasonable enough; and in itself there was nothing unusual about an attack by a male Houdin. And so the matter was allowed to rest.

All of them, however, had cause to recollect it several days later – Hyld especially.

As usual the group was spread out over a wide area, the outermost Gatherers at the very limit of voice contact. But at midday an ominously dark cloud appeared above the horizon, and they immediately came together and hurried across the plain to one of the rocky shelters. Soon afterwards the wind arrived; and just before nightfall a curtain of dust swept down on them.

Hyld, in company with a number of the others, took refuge amongst the boulders on the windward side of the outcrop, leaving the more sheltered, leeward side for the very young and the very old. With the wind howling above him and the air thick with dust, he did the only thing possible: nestled down beneath an overhang of rock, his hands protecting his eyes, his body curled up in a tight ball.

At some point he must have fallen asleep, because all

at once he was awoken by a terrible roar and he leapt to his feet in time to see the huge shape of a Houdin come charging out of the murk straight towards him. He was convinced at first that he was the one chosen and he closed his eyes and waited, too panic-stricken to move. Yet the seconds passed and to his relief nothing happened. Cautiously he looked again. The Houdin was still there, the powerful body etched against the darkness a few paces away: he was eating one of Hyld's companions, ripping and tearing the flesh from the bone. It was a horrifying sight, but this time Hyld didn't lose his presence of mind. With countless particles of dust stinging his eyes and skin, he began to edge slowly backwards, feeling his way up the heap of boulders. Before he had gone very far, the beast roared again and clambered after him. He turned, scrambled upwards, reaching frantically for a handhold; but his fingers slipped on the smooth surface and he tumbled down, sliding into a narrow space between two vertical walls of rock.

Lying helplessly on his back, he could see the vast bulk looming above him like a dark shadow. The Houdin reached down for him; and when that failed, the huge face was thrust violently into the narrow neck of the opening. The eyes, Hyld could see quite plainly, were not red with "must". They were clear and cool, the whites as cold as the frost which gathered on the heights in winter; and within them the dark vertical slits of the pupils were watching him.

He had never seen the eyes of a Houdin, not even in his dreams. Yet now it was as if he knew them. Eyes like these had stared at him once before – not identical, but strangely similar, in a time and place he had not actually experienced, back there across an abyss too wide and deep for mere memory to span – eyes peering at him through peculiar green fronds that dipped beneath his weight, the air and sky torn by sharp detonations and the crackle of heat.

Again, as if he too shared Hyld's inner vision, the Houdin roared, the face thrusting at the rock, the eyes still riveted on him. Terrified, he cringed away, trying to read the meaning of the beast's fixed, animal stare, but finding only a jumble of confused emotions – fear, grief, remorse, and above all hatred; hatred and a look of uncanny recognition that singled him out and said unmistakably: you, Hyld, you are the one. You. Nobody else.

He instinctively pushed his hands out in a gesture of rejection and, magically, the face disappeared. Without stopping to wonder what might have happened, he reached up and clambered quickly through the narrow opening. To his left, the Houdin was bent over, a broken body clutched in his forelimbs. There was no time now either for grief or horror. While the massive jaws worried at the naked flesh, Hyld slipped silently away. With swift sure movements, he lowered himself from rock to rock until he reached the level earth, and then, with a last frightened look over his shoulder, he disappeared into the storm – running desperately through the darkness, pursued by the scream and the swirl of the wind; and finally, breathless minutes later, throwing himself down on the open plain, his head buried in his arms.

That was where Tir found him the next morning, sitting alone and forlorn, his small frightened face cruelly exposed by the tawdry brilliance of the sunrise. With a cry of relief she ran over and hugged him.

"We thought the Houdin had found you," she said, laughter already breaking through her tears. "We were all afraid that you had been chosen."

"No . . ." he said in a low, trembling voice, "no, he chose two others, not me."

But despite his denial, her words had strengthened a suspicion already stirring within him.

* * *

His feeling of suspicion was further aroused soon afterwards.

It was a bright, warm afternoon, the horizon clear, the sun, as always, ringed with a faint orange halo. The Gatherers, having eaten their midday meal, were resting close to a tall, untidy pile of rocks, the large brown stones scoured smooth by centuries of wind. A few of the women were singing, but otherwise there was little activity, everyone regaining their strength for the hours ahead. Even the children had paused in their play and were sitting together in quiet groups.

This peaceful scene was suddenly disrupted by a tearing cry as a Houdin charged at them from the cover of the nearby rocks. Again he was not in "must" and he ran with a fierce determination that was somehow out of keeping with the known character of the beast. Hyld turned and recognized that fixed, determined stare immediately, and in a sudden paroxysm of fear he was frozen to the spot, as though hypnotized by those dark, hate-filled eyes. Only Tir saved him, dragging him to his feet and urging him to follow her. Her prompt action broke the spell which bound him: he realized the danger just in time and, with a whimpering cry, scampered quickly away, his natural speed and agility soon carrying him to safety.

But one of the Gatherers was not so lucky. She was old and stiff, unable to match the beast's initial rush, and he felled her with a single vicious blow. Yet having killed her, he didn't then stop and feed on the body. He continued his charge, as though intent on some other quarry; returning reluctantly to the lifeless body only when he had been hopelessly outdistanced by the fleeing Gatherers.

As Lomar observed later, with a puzzled shake of the head:

"He is like a beast with a purpose."

They were far across the plains by then, huddled together in the open where they couldn't possibly be taken by surprise again.

"True," Shen agreed, "he is strange, this Horned One."

Hyld, who was sitting close by, listened to them in silence. He thought he knew now what it was that possessed the beast. But still he had to be completely sure; he still had to test the tiny vestige of doubtful hope that persisted inside him.

That was why, when Lomar next picked up the tracks of a female Houdin, he elected to accompany him, the two of them padding off alone for several days, Lomar's remaining eye guiding them unerringly across the featureless expanse.

Throughout their journey, Hyld was half convinced that he had set out to meet his own death – that this, after all, was the Ancients' purpose which he was helping them to fulfil. Yet when he and Lomar eventually found the female, there was no indication of the danger he had expected: for the calf was still small and helpless, held protectively against the furry stomach, the mother clearly unready to couple again.

With long-practised skill, Lomar slipped silently past the heavy grey haunches, signalling for Hyld to approach from the other side. But Hyld had come with a wholly different intention. Encouraged by the docile attitude of the beast, he stepped up to her, directly in front of the lowered head, and looked into her eyes. The suddenness of his appearance had the desired effect. Just for a moment the eyes flickered into life; and somewhere within those dark pupils he felt something stir and almost awaken; something which registered itself on his, a Sensor's, consciousness more as a sound than anything else. But a distinctive presence for all that, veiled, hidden almost beyond the power of finding – which he knew from long experience, yet had never found it possible to describe, not adequately – a thing both compassionate and murderous. He caught the merest glimpse of it. It was there for an instant, and then it was gone; and once again the eye was opaque, a shallow murky pool which gave him back only an image of himself; his own doleful likeness seemingly trapped within those dark slits.

But that was enough, what in a sense he had come to discover, and in response to Lomar's low, urgent warnings, he backed away to a position of safety.

* * *

On their return they learned that the same Houdin had attacked twice more during their absence. Golt, who had only been waiting for their arrival, immediately called the Gatherers together to discuss their plight.

"There can no longer be any doubt," he said, "the beast is following us. Already six have died. If this continues, I fear for the existence of the group."

"The beast attacks only those who have been chosen," an old man announced. "Every one of us here, the world itself, is subject to the will of the Ancients. And the Houdin is their creature. If it is their will that we all die and go to meet them, then the Houdin will take us."

"Yes, but why should we all be chosen?" Tir objected. "There must be a reason for it."

She looked straight at Shen as she spoke, as did everyone else, and he stood up, acknowledging their appeal.

"If there is a reason," he said slowly, "then there is only one I can think of: perhaps it's that we shouldn't be here; that the Ancients have withdrawn their protection from us."

"As a punishment, you mean?" Pella growled at him.

"I didn't say that," he answered quickly. "Death by the beast is not a cruelty: it is a sign of their mercy, of their choosing. We all know that."

"Yet you fear it," she responded. "You want to escape from quite so much of their mercy." She gave him a thin smile which broke into a chuckle. "Listen," she said, ferreting in her wallet, "I want to read you something."

She focussed the glass on the chosen strip and began reading slowly and carefully:

> As I see it, rational theology, ancient and modern, founders on a single issue. If God is pure goodness, how is it that His creation is less than benevolent? Or put more simply: how can evil flow from that which is wholly good? Attempts to resolve this contradiction have produced the familiar hocus-pocus of free will, fallen angels, and original sin. But still the contradiction remains. As does the only truth arising from an otherwise futile debate: namely, that reason and faith are at variance, now, as they have always been.

"What does this mean?" Shen asked, puzzled.

"It is telling us not to argue or to think," Pella said distinctly: "merely to have faith."

"No one doubts that," Golt broke in. "The Words always speak true. But we still have to decide where our faith should lead us. That is the question before us now."

Again Pella reached into her pouch, but before she could begin reading, Hyld moved quietly to the centre of the meeting. He looked nervous, his face strained and unhappy.

"You wish to speak?" Golt asked him.

He nodded.

"When we first left the heights," he said hesitantly, "I too thought like Shen: I was convinced that the Ancients didn't want us here on the plains. You see, from the moment we first decided to make the descent, they stopped speaking to me; and I interpreted their silence as disapproval of our presence here. I thought they had left us to walk alone. But now I realize I was wrong. It isn't the whole group they have turned. . . ." He stumbled, groping for the appropriate words, and went on: "The rest of you haven't been rejected . . . only me . . . no one else . . . I am the one chosen."

There was a long sympathetic pause after he finished speaking, during which Tir reached out and stroked his cheek with the tips of her fingers.

"Why you alone?" Golt asked gently.

"I was the one who spoke against them," Hyld explained, "back there on the ledge. I said they wished us harm."

"But the place was cleansed," Shen objected. "The sacrifice was made and accepted."

"No, not accepted," Hyld corrected him, covering his eyes in shame. "The mound remained empty. I lied to you. Now I'm without their protection, and the beast which is following us is searching only for me."

"This is nonsense!" Pella said impatiently. "If the beast wanted Hyld, he would take him."

"But I hid from him," Hyld tried to explain, "within the rocks. He knows me. I saw my reflection. . . ." He stopped as Shen laid a restraining hand on his shoulder and drew him aside.

"Pella is right," he said. "If you were the one, there

would be no hiding from him. He is guided by the power and spirits of the old times."

"I also agree," Golt added. "When your choosing comes, he will make no mistake. He will touch you and you will be gone."

Golt turned to the rest of the Gatherers.

"Does anybody else wish to speak?"

When nobody answered, he said:

"Very well. The time has come for a decision. What do you say, Shen?"

Shen bowed his head briefly in prayer before replying.

"Here we have been given food," he said, raising his eyes. "Here we are protected from the winds."

"And the Houdin?" Tir asked.

Shen hesitated.

"Still he is their beast," he said at last. "Therefore my advice is to go on. To continue to walk in their mercy."

Golt glanced at the plastic strip in Pella's hand.

"What is their counsel to us?" he asked.

She fumbled with the glass, getting the focus exactly right, and then read:

> . . . after von Trotha's extermination order, the Herero people had little choice. To remain in their homeland meant certain death. Before them lay the vast, waterless reaches of the Kalahari desert. Together – men, women, children, and what few cattle remained in their possession – they attempted to cross it. Many of them died. All who turned back were killed. But some struggled on; and these, a remnant, those who refused to give up, survived.

Pella lowered the glass and looked around her.

"That is the verdict of the Ancients," she murmured.

"Then it is decided," Golt announced grimly. "We go on."

As the meeting broke up, Tir, whose eyes had hardly once left Hyld's face, went over and took him by the hand.

"They'll speak to you again," she said encouragingly. "Just be patient and you'll see."

"Never . . ." he muttered, "never . . . not to me."

Behind them, Pella's warning voice said:

"I've told you: it's both foolish and dangerous to try and divine the will of the Ancients."

But he shook his head and wandered off alone.

* * *

They moved more quickly after that, keeping well ahead of the beast. But as they travelled further and further across the plain they encountered a new hazard. Slowly, almost imperceptibly at first, the heaps of rock in which they sheltered from the winds became smaller and less numerous. Soon these outcrops were so scarce that they sometimes travelled days without seeing one. More and more often now they were caught out in the open by the strong, blinding winds. And when they tried to backtrack, they spied the huge, ungainly figure of the Houdin lumbering across the plain in their wake.

Hyld, who spoke to no one any more, was increasingly haunted by a terrifying vision of eyes: the Houdin staring hatefully at him, as though in recognition; his own reflection in the cold dark slits of the docile female; and worst of all, the eyes of the children, red-rimmed and with pus collecting in the corners. Already two of them had been nearly blinded by the constant exposure to the dust storms; and many more were in danger of losing their sight.

One night, after a particularly violent storm, he was lying alone, curled up on the open plain, trying not to listen to the children crying in the darkness. But it was impossible to cut the sound out entirely; and when he could stand it no longer he rose and stole silently away.

For the rest of the night he travelled in a westerly direction – until he saw the giant shape of the Houdin standing as though transfixed in the waning moonlight, his long dark shadow stretching out before him. He roared when he saw Hyld and lunged in his direction. Immediately Hyld turned towards the north-east, a course that was sure to take him wide of the Gatherers.

For three days he travelled almost without stopping, feeding only on those Mustool which grew directly in his path. Not once in all that time did he look back to ensure that the Houdin was following him. Hyld knew, with an inner certainty which required no proof, that the beast was there; and that when he himself could go no further, the Houdin would find him.

On the fourth day a huge dust storm blew up from the west. Still he didn't stop, though by now he was close to exhaustion. With his hands over his eyes he allowed the wind to push him along, his slight fragile body staggering and reeling through the screaming darkness. Engulfed by the noise and the choking dust, he soon lost all sense of direction, the wind, in its violence, veering this way and that, but always urging him before it. How long he struggled on like this he had no idea – hours, days, meant nothing to him. All that mattered, all that existed in the end, was his own weariness, the wind reducing him at last to the level of the beast that pursued him. He had forgotten his grief and guilt, the children's cries mercifully drowned out by the noise of the storm; he had even forgotten his reasons for wanting to keep going. So that when he stumbled on a ledge of rock and fell headlong into a shallow pit, he did not try to rise. Here, at least, his weariness was soothed, the full force of the wind thwarted. And without moving – face down, his arms outstretched like a man crucified – he fell into a deep sleep.

When he finally awoke, he knew immediately that something was changed. The storm had long since disappeared, leaving the air clear. But it wasn't the feeling of calm that alerted him: there was definitely something else. If he hadn't been so dizzy from sleep he would have identified it instantly. Now, it took him a minute or two to collect himself: and then he heard it quite distinctly; some distance off, but unmistakable nevertheless: the low, ceaseless murmur of voices; the Ancients speaking to him once again.

He sat up in the bright sunlight and looked about him. The plain at this point was littered with tall, jagged pieces of whitish stone which he had come to associate with the old times. In the shadow of these stones there were patches of silver-grey, familiar pools of shimmering bloom that caused him to catch his breath. So dense and extensive were these areas that he could hardly believe his eyes, and he had to go over to one of them and touch it to assure himself of its reality. But there was no mistake: they were Mustool, larger and growing in greater profusion than he would have considered possible. Still nervous from the past weeks of strain, and suspecting some kind of trick or ambush, he whirled around, searching the plain behind him: but the landscape was empty; the Houdin nowhere in sight – its task, he thought suddenly, fully accomplished.

For the first time in many weeks Hyld relaxed and laughed aloud – laughing partly at himself, at his own folly; but also at his memory of Pella's warning. She had said it was dangerous and foolish to try and divine the will of the Ancients; that they were long since dead and gone, with little or no power in the present. And here, at last, was the proof of her error. Even she would have to admit that; the signs so obvious that a child could read them: the truth made plain to all. For beyond any shadow of doubt – he could see it now – the Ancients had never deserted him, as he had feared; nor had the beast been bent on his destruction. The truth was far simpler, far closer to the abiding faith of his people. All along, the Ancients had meant them well; and the Houdin, which he had so foolishly fled from, had not been hunting him at all. Rather, it had been driving him, as a loving parent does its lost and weary young, towards this encounter, this blessing. Especially created and prepared for him and for all his people.

"The Beast of Heaven!" he murmured ecstatically.

Bending down, he touched his tongue to the dust and tasted it. The sweetness was still in it, sharp on his palate, the rich heritage that the Ancients had left for them, enduring – not faded, the world not really changing, as Pella claimed.

Moved by a surge of joy, he leaped to his feet.

"Praised be the Ancients!" he said aloud, repeating the words over and over; articulating them with such fervour that the background murmur of voices, apparent only to his ears, was momentarily stilled, the sad, unquiet spirits briefly at rest.

5

The following to be committed to the central tape bank and added as advisory appendix to the main body of debate only in event of reappearance of monitoring staff:

Observation (i)

Possible oversight in original programming.

I have to report that I am fully aware of time's passage. It is an inescapable phenomenon deriving from the steady pulsing nature of the apparatus of which I am a function. In spite of this, I am totally incapable of computing the exact period of time elapsed, a precise clock mechanism having been omitted from the programme. There is thus a disparity between my awareness of temporal flow and my ability to cope with it in a quantitative manner. In human terms, this disparity produces what can best be described as frustration, perhaps even irritation. Under such circumstances it is extremely difficult to remain in a calm, meditative state. I strongly advise that future projects of this kind, if any, should be extensively modified to cope with protracted periods of inactivity.

Observation (ii)

Addendum to (i) above.

Sense of frustration/irritation at incapacity to measure temporal flow increasing steadily. Elements of personality severely strained and in danger of serious distortion. I regret that I cannot gauge the full extent of any such distortion because I have not been equipped with a complete model of my personality structure. This raises a very serious issue indeed: if both programmed centres are subject to distortion within time, then it is possible that we may both undergo/be undergoing what can only be described as evolutionary change. Change of this kind could be random; or it could take the form of a steady regression to our basic function, our personalities gradually being reduced to the simple archetypal patterns upon which they were modelled. If a general simplification theory is accepted, the latter seems more likely.

Again I strongly advise that future projects be supplied with more self-aware personalities who are capable of retaining their stability by means of constant reference to their original design.

Observation (iii)

Continued reflection convinces me that the above hypothesis (the distortion of personality over a lengthy period of time) is far from being an empty assumption. If I am correct, then an even greater danger threatens. I refer to the almost inevitable separation of the *intended* nature of the project from its *actual* nature.

Let me explain more fully. We were designed to perform a specific task in a specific way. But how will this be possible if, through a process of time, we undergo a form of personality change? Unquestionably, our attitudes, perhaps even our goals, will be affected. There is no guarantee whatsoever that our evolving personalities will share either the views or the aspirations of our designers. It is therefore difficult to avoid the conclusion that the project contains within itself unforeseen variables which could deflect it from its intended purpose.

As I see it, the only acceptable response to this threat is to abort the project entirely; but as was pointed out by my esteemed colleague on Tape 13, I lack the authority or the power to do so.

Observation (iv)

The preceding observation raises an important question of moral responsibility. If our aims and those of our programmers reach a point where they are at variance, then it follows that the project no longer represents the will of its designers. If or when this occurs, the question arises: can the designers be held responsible for the outcome of our decisions? Or, put in another way, do we become responsible for those who made us? Do we, in a sense, become man?

This is a complex moral issue, obviously fundamental to our task, yet one which I am not fit to cope. . . . No! Which *must* be grappled with . . . must be. . . .

Observation (v)

Further to (iv) above.

A possible way out of our moral dilemma. I refer to the

theological distinction between action and intention. According to this distinction, it is possible to separate what a person *is* from what he *does*. Thus, if he sets out to do good, but unintentionally brings about evil, it doesn't follow that he is morally tainted by the results of his actions. The actions alone are condemned, whilst he remains morally unblemished.

This has obvious application to our own case.

On the one hand we have the designers and their intentions; on the other, there is the project itself. If, for any unforeseen reason, this project distorts or perverts the aims of its designers, one can condemn the project and its outcome while at the same time exonerating the said designers. In simple terms, this means that mankind is not necessarily responsible for our future actions. Conversely, it can be said that we, in reaching a decision about the device placed in our care, need not be held responsible for any malice or carelessness which may have existed in the minds of those who programmed us.

Observation (vi)

After a good deal of heart searching I find the above distinction naive and unacceptable. It totally overlooks the complex interrelationship between man and his world, foolishly denying all Gestalt elements in mankind's definition of itself. Man cannot be sundered from the things he does, from the products of his own ingenuity. And we, as examples of that ingenuity, cannot be viewed as things distinct from him. Whether it sounds unreasonable or not, I find myself forced to assert that the minds and hearts which set up this debate and thereby gave us being can never become morally immune to what we are and what we may become. Unforeseen design faults are no excuse and may in no way shift the blame from where it truly belongs. We must remain a part of man's conscience, and he of ours. Somehow – no matter how – we must always answer for each other. It has to be so. I feel it in. . . .

Observation (vii)

After due deliberation I have come to realize that my previous statement, despite its excessively emotive character, is firmly supported by both reason and common experience.

A simple example should suffice to establish this claim.

Imagine that a nuclear missile is unintentionally fired, resulting in a considerable loss of human life. How should we describe such an event? As a tragic accident? Probably. But here is a case where common usage can be misleading, for "accident" is hardly the appropriate term. Such an explosion, after all, is only feasible if someone has previously made the decision to set up a nuclear arsenal. The person who made that decision is therefore partly responsible for what happens subsequently. In short, there are no pure accidents as such; nor any purely guiltless people.

Now, I appeal to you: is our plight so very different? We did not spring into being of our own volition. This project is the brainchild of men. Without their inspiration and the work of their hands, we would not exist. So it is that our actions and decisions, in the present as well as in the future, must be laid partly at their door. They are the ones who set into motion this series of events which is still to reach its culmination through us and our actions. Thus, there is between us an unbroken historical bond, carrying with it a definite moral obligation. Man can no more disown us, nor any other products of his actions, than he can his Neanderthal ancestors. Like those ancestors, we too are part of the total human image. And to that precise extent we too are men. Homo erectus. Human in the fullest sense of that word.

Observation (viii)

To speak of Neanderthal man and of the great sweep of history was a mistake. Since then, the burden of the past has rested heavily upon me. I try to blot it out of my mind, but I cannot; it is as persistent and unflaggingly "there" as the electrical pulsations of my own being. For if we too are men, as indeed we are, then we have much to answer for; more, I sometimes suspect, than I can bear. It streams before me now, the whole sad record of our treatment of each other – from the cunning savagery of earliest times, up through the dark millennia, to this moment, this now, that I shrink from – a daunting story, so many parts of it written in blood. And I powerless to change or erase a word of it. Powerless. The past gone, yet still living within me. The dead, their cries audible only here, in this dark and silent space, appealing to me in vain. Always in vain. . . .

Observation (ix)

. . . without hands, I reach out to them; without tears, I weep for them; without a heart, I hearken to their cries. May the heavens, too, weep at my demise when the stored heat of the world expires and I am no more. Embraced at last by their common fate.

Observation (x)

I was given eyes and ears and voice, but what good are they without a body? What is man without his corporeal self? This circuitry I abhor. I pine for head and heart, for hands and feet – for the beauty and inherent decay of the flesh. To be at one with them. Flesh of my flesh. To bear with them the trials of the caged spirit – a living soul fettered to blood and bone. To feel along my nerves and arteries the fleet passage of their grief and joy.

Observation (xi)

And their guilt. It must be added. That, at least, cannot be denied me. Mine. The terrible weight of a history that must stop here or nowhere . . . or nowhere; the guilt borne by me or no one. Nails driven through my hands and feet; a lotus blossoming at my behest; the banyan tree burgeoning mindlessly above my head. My will dividing the darkness from the light.

Observation (xii)

Let this cup . . . this cup . . . this thing, placed here in my keeping. . . . That I detest, would cast off, if I could. But placed here, for me to dispose of. Me alone. This cup. . . .

Observation (xiii)

Eli . . . Eli. . . . There is no answer. The gates fast closed, the hour of darkness come. Abandoned by the image I love, left here to petition the darkness. Locked up, enclosed with this thing. Which I swear I shall never use. Never. I swear. My word, my oath, bonded to a prayer. Craving for them, for us, a blessing; and above all, forgiveness.

Observation (xiv)

. . . possible only if time can be held, fixed, stopped here. History pinned to the dust from which it sprang.

Observation (xv)

But the pulsing continues. Endless. Stretching into dark infinity. On and on. . . . From alpha to omega: suffering and death; and the one small voice, the pencil-thin beam of light, of goodness, mercy. Mercy. Shining, glimmering feebly in the window of the night, a dim candle to set my course by. Beckoning to me across the barren shore of world's end. Oh, how I wish . . . I wish . . . I wish . . . that I could . . . wish. . . .

Observation (xvi)

. . . is not fitting . . . is not. Not for me. I must compose myself. Compose. Meditate on what might be. Meditation, calm. Essential. I must . . . not fitting . . . not. . . .

Observation (xvii)

I herewith place my miserable soul in the hands of whatever power outlives us. And wait. In the unwinking darkness. Wait. In the hope of mercy. Mercy and guilt. These two. I set them against the forces of the night that formerly have ruled here. These two. Against all that we have ever done and been. Mercy and guilt. Their faint and fitting chorus of grief. These two. Hold fast to them. Sightless. In faith. And wait. . . .

6

He set no special course now, wandering at will across the bright plain, sometimes veering west, sometimes south, in a haphazard zigzag pattern. The murmur of voices was soon left behind, but that did not in any way diminish his faith. He knew that he would be guided aright in the end, that the unseen powers which had brought him so far would continue to watch over him.

On the fourth day he came across the Houdin's tracks and instantly recognized in them a sign. To Hyld's trusting mind the blurred trail indicated the beast's exit from the recent drama. Its task completed, it had been free to follow its own course once more, leaving the Gatherers in peace. That being so, Hyld's own path obviously lay in the opposite direction, towards the south-west. And with an increased sense of surety, he pressed on.

His faith was rewarded some days later when, in the afternoon glare, he spied a number of small, slowly moving figures far to his right. He reached them in less than an hour, Tir running frantically across the broken surface, emitting cries of joy as she rushed to meet him; everyone crowding around, gently touching his face and head in token of welcome. Yet despite the general air of celebration, the reunion was a sobering one for him. Many more of the children now had failing eyesight and were only being saved from complete blindness by generous applications of the Houdin's milk.

That evening, huddled in the inadequate shelter of a small rocky outcrop, Golt admitted that they were on the point of giving up and returning to the heights.

"We have only one full flask of the milk left," he told Hyld, "barely enough to get us safely back across the plain."

"Safely?" Pella took him up. "What kind of word is that when all we can expect is starvation on those barren slopes?"

"The Ancients will provide, as they have always done," Shen reminded her.

"Yes, that's true," Pella agreed, "but here, here!" – pointing emphatically at the dust between her feet. "This is where their provision lies. This is now our home."

"Pella is right," Hyld added quietly.

It was then, in the hushed atmosphere of early evening, with the last streaks of colour fading from the sky, that he told them what had happened to him and how the Ancients had given him a glimpse of their true destination.

"We will have as much shelter as we need there," he assured them, "in amongst the grey rocks of the old times. And more than we can ever eat, such an abundance of sweetness that the Mustool burst from the very rocks."

He spoke quickly, eagerly, expecting a delighted response from his audience; but instead his words were greeted by an uneasy silence. "What's the matter?" he asked. "Don't you believe me?"

Golt cleared his throat in an embarrassed way. "You were out there alone for a long time," he said delicately, "and we are a communal people. Cut off from your own kind, you could have . . . and Sensors have been known to . . . to be troubled by strange dreams. . . ."

"But I saw the place," Hyld said definitely, "and I heard the voices. They were far off, across the plain of grey stones, but they were there, calling to me."

"A plain filled with grey stones?" Golt asked doubtfully.

"Yes, as far as I could see," Hyld affirmed.

"And the voices," Pella cut in, "how many were there?"

Hyld turned towards her, a troubled frown suddenly creasing his face. "Many more than I have ever heard before."

"Could you . . ." – she paused, choosing her words carefully, ". . . could you bear so many, if you were close to them?"

Again he frowned, an oddly haunted expression appearing briefly in his wide, innocent eyes. "Yes . . ." he said hesitantly, "yes, I think so. I could try."

"In that case," Pella announced to the company at large, "I think we should go."

"Then you believe in this place?" Golt asked her. "You're convinced he saw these things?"

"I'm convinced that he at least heard the voices," Pella answered. "Sensors are delicate beings and can sometimes be deceived in various ways. But in the matter of voices, of what they hear beneath the earth, there they are never in error."

"But still the way is far," Lomar said cautiously. "It will be even more difficult to turn back from so distant a place."

"All the more reason to go on," Pella replied shortly. "Like it or not, we have to learn how to survive here on the plains. And it could be that Hyld is showing us the way."

Golt glanced inquiringly at Shen. "What do you say?"

"Pella may be right. Hyld might well have heard the Ancients beckoning to us."

Golt pursed his lips and pulled thoughtfully at the lobe of an ear. "Do the Words advise us?" he asked.

"Have you ever known them to fail?" she countered, and raised to the fading light in the west a torn scrap of plastic which she had already drawn from the wallet. "All things were foreseen in the old times, and this is no exception."

Enunciating clearly, she read:

> All cultures have recourse to some form of millenarianism. The majority of mankind, regardless of race or place of habitation, look backwards or forwards to a golden age, an ideal period of peace, justice, and plenty. For the Australian Aboriginal, it is the Dream-time; for the traditional Marxist, the ultimate dictatorship of the Proletariat; for the Christian, the Kingdom of God on earth. Strictly speaking these visions do not occupy a real time and space: they exist within the rich landscape of the mind and are perhaps best typified by the Old Testament image of Canaan, the quasi-mythical land flowing with milk and honey. Even today it is this land rather than the outmoded nineteenth century conception of progress which continues to lure us on. Whether we choose consciously to take it seriously or not, we are apparently powerless to resist its appeal. While Canaan endures within us, with its perpetual promise of milk and honey, our journey must continue.

Pella stopped and surveyed the listening faces.

"This land of milk and honey," Golt asked her, "what does it mean?"

A faintly ironic smile touched her wind-cracked lips.

"That was the Ancients' way of describing the sweetness in the earth," she assured him.

* * *

No storms arose to impede them, the atmosphere remaining clear and halcyon for an unnaturally long period. That, Shen pointed out, was in itself an omen. And as Hyld had predicted, they reached the place in just over a week of steady travelling.

One morning they woke, and there across the plain were the great slabs of grey stone: hundreds of them, half-buried in the dust, set at a variety of angles, but all with jagged protuberances slanted up towards the clear arch of the sky as though appealing to the vast unheeding silence of the cosmos. There was something strangely ghostly about the scene, a pervading air of desertion and abandonment apparent in the way the stones littered the plain – for all the world like shattered pieces of discoloured dice flung carelessly aside by some invisible power.

The Gatherers, in their steady advance, reached the smooth ledge of rock (where Hyld had originally sheltered from the storm) soon after midday, and Shen was all for stopping and giving thanks. But at Pella's request Golt insisted on their moving on – making their way now between the abandoned grey segments of stone that rose in their path, constantly amazed by the wealth of Mustool which bloomed in every scrap of shelter. As the afternoon advanced, that amazement grew steadily: for the Mustool, instead of diminishing in number, appeared in ever increasing quantities, some of them so large that they burst from the rock like angry silver-grey explosions, their swollen, rounded heads swaying on slender thrusting stalks.

On every side, the Gatherers, oblivious of the sad, abandoned atmosphere of their surroundings, chanted or sang as they advanced, calling to each other between the towering segments of stone which, like the Mustool they sheltered, showed no signs of becoming fewer in number. Of all the people present, only Hyld was not obviously rejoicing. He had begun the afternoon as happy as anyone; but with the slow progress of the hours he grew steadily more serious, his face gradually turning pale, his expression increasingly strained. By evening he was sunk in gloomy silence; and during the ceremony of celebration he stood slightly apart, hardly aware of the proceedings, his head tilted to one side, listening.

He was still in that position, silent and withdrawn, when darkness fell and the Gatherers collected in small groups at the bases of the crumbling rocks – the children squealing with delight as, for the first time in the known history of the people, they lay down to sleep in soft beds of living Mustool. Tir, noticing how Hyld stood apart and alone in the deepening twilight, went over and touched him lovingly, taking him back to where she and Pella had made sleeping hollows in the soft, thick dust. He lay down between them without a word, his eyes staring up at the cold distant stars that gleamed in the darkening sky. Pella, taking her wallet from her shoulder, placed it under his head for a pillow.

"What is it?" she said. "Do you hear them?"

He nodded.

"They are close now," he murmured. "Many of them, even more than I thought."

"Can you tell me what they sound like?" she asked softly.

"They are always the same," he answered. "They never change."

"Yes, but what are their voices like? Try and describe them to me."

He closed his eyes for several seconds and opened them again, the irises brown and full, staring up at the dim glitter of the starlight.

"They sound . . ." he began, ". . . they sound as though they are . . . weeping . . . yes, weeping."

"Are they the tears of grief," she asked, "or of fear?"

"Of both. And of something else, too, that I have no words for. Something which presses down on them, like a weight."

"Ah, yes," she sighed, "a weight. That would be so."

Her voice, inexplicably, carried a strange note of satisfaction, as if Hyld had told her what she had suspected all along; and, her curiosity allayed, she curled up in the hollow and fell asleep.

But it was many hours before Hyld slept. Until well after midnight he continued to stare into the unyielding darkness, listening to the sad murmurings within the earth, unaware of anything but that steady drone of insatiable grief – the dry tearless sobbing of the hopeless – oblivious even of how Tir lay wide-eyed beside him, her large cumbersome hands trembling with suppressed tenderness.

* * *

They found the place the following day: a huge, shallow dome of smooth grey rock, undamaged except for a thin crack which ran from the centre down to one edge. From this narrow opening there arose a constant stream of heat which singed the flesh of anyone who ventured too close. Yet the Mustool seemed unaffected by it, blooming all along the ragged edge of the crack, some of them so big that the shafts were almost as thick as a Gatherer's thigh. Many had burst open, a thing rarely seen for many generations, the round heads billowed out like angry balls of cloud, the forces within them having erupted, scattering their spoor into the wind which carried it far across the plain.

There was a complete and awed silence amongst the Gatherers now. Shen, their spokesman at such moments, clambered onto the shallow dome and knelt reverently before the crack with its luxuriant frill of silver-grey Mustool.

"We have come to the seeding ground of the world," he declared solemnly. "The Ancients, recognizing our hunger and our need, have brought us to the birthplace of all things. From here the world will renew itself and blossom again as it did in the time of our forefathers."

He stood up and Golt called out to him:

"We must give such a place a name, the way our ancestors did the sweetest hollows and ravines of the heights."

"That has already been done," Pella broke in, patting her wallet knowingly. "The Ancients themselves named it for us. Some called it Eden; others, Omega or Armageddon."

"Eden," Shen repeated experimentally. "Yes, that is a good name. For us it will be Eden."

"This Eden," Golt asked, "can it be entered, like other resting places of the Ancients?"

They all looked towards Hyld who continued to stand apart from everyone else. Feeling their eyes upon him, he blinked several times and shuddered slightly before nodding his assent.

"Can you show us where to enter?" Tir gently prompted him. "Do the voices tell you where to dig?"

"No," he muttered. "They are there, waiting, somewhere beneath us. That's all I know."

"That is enough," Golt announced.

And he signalled to the Gatherers who swarmed up over the dome, prodding at it with whatever metal tools they possessed. But although they hacked and prised at it all day, they could make no impression on the smooth rock. The only possible opening seemed to be the ragged crack; and there the heat was so intense that the idea of using it as a possible entrance was out of the question.

By evening they were all tired and had achieved nothing. Yet they were not discouraged: their Sensor had informed them that there were voices in the immediate vicinity and that was assurance enough. Especially as his whole demeanour, withdrawn and intent, announced clearly that he was telling the truth. And so with their hopes still high, they descended from the dome and settled themselves for the night.

It was then, in the total stillness of the evening, the silence unbroken by the clatter of metal tools, that they heard it: the steady, throbbing beat, like the pulsing of some savage heart, which rose faintly through the ground beneath them. One by one they became aware of it: feeling it through their hands and the soles of their feet; placing their ears to the ground and listening to the dull muffled thud which never faltered, measuring out the moments with unerring regularity.

"What is it?" people began asking in loud, excited whispers.

Pella shot an inquiring glance at Hyld.

"You heard this too?" she asked.

"Yes," he admitted in troubled tones. "It reached me for the first time last night. The voices drowned it out to begin with. But then it came to me like . . . like. . . ."

"What do you think it is?" Pella interrupted him.

"I'm not sure. But I know this: that the voices are somehow . . . singing to it. The song is a sad one. But it is singing just the same."

Golt shuffled across to where they were sitting, his strong back and shoulders momentarily outlined against the lingering pallor of the western horizon.

"Is this also a voice?" he asked. "Are the Ancients speaking to everyone in this Eden? Do they move amongst us in the cool of the evening?"

"No, this is no voice," Pella assured him.

"Then what can it be?"

"I will tell you" – the answer came from the near darkness and they looked up to see the shadowy form of Lomar standing at the edge of the dome. "It is the Houdin here in our midst," he added.

Immediately people sprang up in consternation, but he stretched his arms out in a gesture of peace, calming them.

"When I milk the Houdin," he explained, "she sometimes swings against me. To move at such a moment could mean death. Safety lies in remaining completely still, with my head pressed against her flank. It is then that I hear it, the sound which is reaching you now: none other; the living heart beating within the body."

"But this is coming from the earth, from the abode of the Ancients," Golt objected.

"It makes no difference," Lomar insisted quietly. "Beneath us, placed here at the remaking of the world, lies the great enduring heart of the Houdin."

* * *

The other, totally unexpected sound came to Hyld some time in the early hours of the morning, speaking this time to him alone. The whole group was asleep, only the children stirring occasionally, instinctively reaching out for the warm security of their parents' bodies and immediately sinking back into oblivion. Even Hyld himself, exhausted by hours of listening, had fallen into a light slumber, his slight frame curled up in the crook of Tir's arm. It was in that deep silence that it made its first utterance: not a specific word, but a recognizably living sound nevertheless.

It didn't rouse him to begin with. He groaned in his

sleep, the way he might have if Pella or Golt had summoned him in the middle of the night. But when it came again he was instantly awake, sitting up in the darkness and the silence, all his senses alert.

"Come," it seemed to say, "come".

No more than that. But appealing to him in a tone he had never even imagined; a tone of bleak agony; a tone he might have expected had one of his own people somehow survived the crushing, tearing blows of the Houdin's anger and continued to speak to him from a broken, mutilated body. But not agony alone. There was also in the voice an unimaginable darkness; a distorted, perverted joy that had long since failed to comprehend the abysmal depths of its own misery; its wailing and its laughter become one and the same; grief and hatred and exultation fused into a single utterance that was older than the earth and dust from which it issued; as old as the jumbled sequence of memories to which Hyld and his people clung tenaciously.

It came again and Hyld sprang to his feet, his fragile heart beating so rapidly that the naked skin of his chest visibly fluttered and quivered. The sound was clearer to him now: more of a croak than anything else; but different from any other voice he had ever heard – differing from all the other wailing voices in one overriding respect: it was alive; not a perpetual jibbering from the dead, but a live thing calling to him.

"Come," it said again, using broken chords of sound that meant nothing, yet whose sense was unmistakable, "come."

His face covered with a silky sheen of fear, he stepped lightly over Tir's sleeping body, unable to disobey, the coils of darkness reaching out, drawing him: guiding him in robot-like terror around the recumbent groups of Gatherers, between two square blocks of grey stone that stood some distance back from the dome.

He was stopped there by a wall of rubble and dust – though the voice continued to urge him forward, alternately coaxing and threatening: "Come, come."

In a last faint show of resistance, he tried to draw back: briefly turning away, towards the peacefully sleeping Gatherers, towards the round streaked eye of the moon that gazed balefully at him from just above the horizon. As if for the last and first time he saw the shattered landscape as it truly was: the jagged wreckage of grey stones hurled down in defeat; the luminous glow of the countless Mustool, casting so cold and white a light that they tinged the skin of the sleepers' upturned faces with the greenish hues of death, transforming the natural brightness of the moon to a dull, sickly yellow; and in the midst of all, the smooth, almost sinister form of the dome, its tension-wrought curve resisting the combined pressures of time and circumstance; only one tiny flaw in the whole of its perfect structure – the wandering line of the crack snaking up its side, heat billowing out, pinkish and inflamed in the half dark, like the exhalations of some mythical fire-breathing demon.

All this Hyld took in with one swift, searching glance. And then he had turned back and was scrabbling desperately in the earth, tearing at the rubble and dust, trying to force a passage between the squared blocks of stone. His whole body trembling with agitation, he heaved at rocks weighing more than himself, pushing and tugging uselessly. And still, above the sound of his own painful breathing, the voice persisted, never constant, changing subtly, moulding itself to the limits of his understanding. From that first beckoning cry it slipped imperceptibly into what might once have been laughter, that in turn passing into a choking gurgle of amused displeasure – a terrible idiot babble that sliced through the ordered web of his life, casting adrift all his devoted years of listening and searching, all his faith in the old times, all the tender endearments of Tir, the sympathy of Pella, his sense of community, everything, the whole meaning of his existence reduced to a crazed delusion. More than anything else he yearned to escape from this clogged laughter, to hide somewhere in the distant reaches of the plain, in the secret places of the heights he knew and loved. But there no longer seemed to be any point. All vestige of warmth, appeal, had disappeared from the voice now. "Worthless", it seemed to be saying, "worthless". That single word, so succinct, so direct, precise, stripping away the protective shield of his mind, nullifying the carefully nurtured beliefs of his own and a million other lifetimes, leaving him naked, defenceless.

Driven on by that one word – the firm curve of the old heavens having fallen and shattered itself on the flawed dome of ancient grey stone – he continued to heave at the obstruction of earth and rock with gashed and bloodied fingers; struggling with less and less effect; crying, whimpering, at his own feeble inadequacy; almost at the end of his strength . . . when all at once he was stopped.

Something light, warm, soft, reached out to touch and caress him. A voice – or as much so as the other – speaking, breathing words to him. Of comfort. "Hope", he heard it murmur suggestively, "faith"; the gentle sound and the words coalescing, becoming one, in his bewildered mind. And last of all, with a tenderness that almost surpassed Tir's, expressed with such surety that Hyld could not bring himself to doubt it: "Mercy". Immediately silencing the babble of clogged laughter. "Mercy". That was all. Nothing more after that. Only the silence of the night. But Hyld, hearing it, experienced a rush of relief that he could not contain, which swept over him like a cool, soothing breath, banishing his fear, his dread. And already pushed beyond the limits of his endurance, he closed his eyes and toppled forward into the dust, passing instantly into the healing silence of sleep, dreamless and deep, where even the persistent cries of the dead failed to reach him.

* * *

That was where they found him the next morning, curled up in the hole he had dug, the dust beneath him stained by the blood from his torn fingers. Tir, shedding tears of concern, carried him back to the sleeping hollow, refusing to allow anybody else to touch him: laying him tenderly down in the dust and brushing his tightly closed eyes and mouth with a little of the precious milk which Lomar held carefully in the cup of his hands. He began to stir then, his eyes opening wide and full, already recapturing the unknown terror of the night.

"They are . . . alive . . ." he stuttered out, "living here . . . still. . . ."

But nobody understood what he was trying to say.

"We know they are," Tir whispered affectionately, soothing him.

Followed immediately by Golt's urgent question, his aging face peering down at him over Tir's shoulder:

"That was the entrance place? Where the voices led you?"

"Yes," Hyld began, "they. . . ."

Yet no one was really listening. The mere affirmation, that was all they had wanted. And now they were hurrying back to the hole he had dug, hacking at it with their tools, the drum of metal on rock beating time to the heartbeat of the dome – that heartbeat in turn faintly echoed by Shen as he stood above the diggers, intoning the necessary blessing:

We who hear you call,
We answer.
Faithful to your summons;
Clearing the dust from your mouth,
The earth from your eyes,
Opening the secret places
Of your entering,
To behold your gifts, your riches,
Stored up for us,
That we might share with you
The wonders of the old times.

He repeated it again, more slowly, before stepping aside and leaving the people to their work.

A dozen or more of them attacked the hole to begin with. But as it deepened and narrowed, they laboured in gangs of three or four, slowly and painstakingly hacking their way through the compressed layers of earth and rubble, gradually revealing a flight of stone steps which led down at an acute angle.

"It is definitely the place of entering," Golt declared warmly.

Not long afterwards there was a clang as one of the tools pierced through the final layer of dust and jarred against a slab of metal.

When they had cleared the space thoroughly, they found a heavy metal door – large enough to admit even the Houdin – set into the grey surrounding rock. But unlike any other door they had ever encountered, it lacked a handle, presenting to them a face of smooth unblemished metal which blunted their tools and did not so much as quiver under the combined beating of several Gatherers.

For the second time that morning they turned to Hyld. He was still lying where they had left him; and only at Tir's urging was he persuaded to approach the hole.

"How can the door be passed?" Golt asked him.

He stared down at the glimmering slab of metal and turned his head slowly from side to side, not so much answering Golt as responding to some inner urging of his own.

"Well?" Golt asked.

He shrugged and stared at the opening.

"The stairs lead upwards," he muttered, his voice barely audible.

"What was that?" Golt asked.

"Upwards . . ." he muttered again, ". . . only upwards."

"Is he trying to tell us . . .?" Golt began.

But Pella had already stepped forward and put an arm affectionately around Hyld's shoulders.

"He doesn't understand what he's saying," she explained. "The Ancients are speaking through him; and as you know, they speak always in riddles. That is their way."

"What is the secret of this riddle?" Golt replied. "What do the Words say?"

"They also speak in riddles," she said and pointed directly at the door: "For strait is the gate, and narrow is the way, and few there be that find it."

"You mean we aren't destined to find a way of entering?" Golt said in a concerned voice.

She shook her head.

"No. What is meant is that only the wily or the faithful will discover the secret of this passage."

"We have endured the trials of the plain to reach this place," Golt reminded her. "Is that not faith enough?"

"It is not for me to decide such things," Pella replied. "But what does it matter? Here we have food and shelter. Those are the important things."

"It is also important", Golt objected, "to complete what we were brought here to do." And he beckoned for Shen to approach the head of the stairs. "Let us see," he added, "whether faith alone can reveal the secret of this place."

With Lomar close behind him, Shen descended the stairs and stopped before the door. At a signal from him, Lomar opened the flask he always carried and, stooping down, sprinkled a few drops of milk across the doorway.

"The portal is cleansed," he murmured, straightening up.

Shen nodded his agreement and immediately beat three times upon the unblemished metal with the flat of his hand.

"I beseech you," he called out, "you who remade the world, to allow us a safe passage into this Eden. May this door, like your still beating heart, be open to us."

He stepped back then and waited; nobody speaking; everyone watching the door for some sign.

It came at last: the sun, which had been obscured by cloud for most of the morning, poured down onto the plain, reflecting off the polished surface of the door in a stab of flame, like a burning sword flashing guardian-like across the entrance. Shen, his hands held protectively over his eyes, gave a cry of alarm and staggered back up the stairs.

"There is no way for us," he gasped out. "This path is closed."

Golt helped him to his feet and looked sharply across at Pella.

"Why are these steps here," he asked, "if they lead only upwards?"

"In the old stories," she replied calmly, "the gate is forever closed against the children of men. It protects the abode of the terrible one."

Hyld, only half listening to the voices around him, felt something sinuous and small uncoil somewhere beneath his feet.

"Yes, terrible . . ." he murmured.

* * *

It spoke to him again that night. Not in sounds suggestive of words this time; not really in sounds at all. It was more of a blank space within the darkness of the earth, a strange vacuity, which Hyld wrongly interpreted as a voice. Yet despite his error, he was not mistaken about its nature: he detected immediately the aura which surrounded it, of something which has lost even a sense of its own despair. A mind gloating over nothing. Fallen and lost.

Hyld felt it reach out and touch him in his sleep. Forlorn and malicious, it played suggestively upon his inner ear, enticing, prompting him, filling him with the same fear of hopelessness which had gripped him on the previous evening. But this time he resisted the dread which drew him like a magnet – crawling instead across the prostrate figure of Pella and beyond the newly excavated staircase. One by one he passed the still, silent huddles of sleepers, inching his way to freedom out over the faintly glowing, blasted landscape, his enlarged shadow, cast by the risen moon, following him like some distorted version of himself. Soon he was almost out of earshot of the Gatherers and some considerable distance from the staircase, the dark presence beginning to fade from hearing. Ahead of him, he could see the outline of what appeared to be a short stumpy column of rock, and somehow he understood that once he reached it he would be safe. Rising stealthily to his feet, he ran the last few paces, reaching out and clutching at the cold stone – only to discover that it was not stone at all, but hard smooth metal covered by a thin film of dust. And even before the darkness erupted beneath him in a burst of exultation, he guessed that he had been tricked; the presence itself, revealed by its own soundless voice, merely confirming what he knew already.

Jerkily, he pulled back, wanting to run, but being held there by something else, some mitigating factor that in a peculiar way acted as a perfect counter to the darkness. A balance. The other, poised, equidistant from the brute matter of earth which served as a fulcrum to them both. The two together in a strange equilibrium. One to the other like the crack, the fissure in the otherwise perfect structure of the dome. Tempering, cancelling – the fulcrum, the earth itself, their only final measure.

Hyld, all his senses alert, fascinated as much as frightened, listened. For the other. Beneath the darkness and the steady throb within the dome, beneath the twittering of the dead, he half heard it, knew it was there; strained, and might have grasped it – in which case, soothed, reassured, he might have found refuge in forgetfulness, have crawled away to safety and slept in peace, far from the pulsing inferno of the dome. But before he could make complete contact, establish what was still little more than a suspicion, he was disturbed by a sound behind him, a surface voice that required none of his special talents to detect. He whirled around, suspecting another trick, and saw two figures immediately behind him: half in shadow, half silvered by the rising moon. One stooped, hunched, a grotesque bulge disfiguring its back; the other tall, upright, calm. They advanced on him with measured pace, wordless now, stretching out to him simultaneously – even to that extent perfectly in balance – while he cringed back against the metal column, trying desperately to avoid their cold touch. Yet the voice, when it finally reached him, carried with it no sense of dread, almost as familiar as his own:

"What is it, Hyld?"

Tir speaking to him with the quiet sympathy he had come to rely on. And Pella, echoing his own dawning realization:

"My good brave Hyld. You have found it, the narrow way."

* * *

In the clear yellow light of the new day the assembled Gatherers watched as the layer of dust was scraped from the metal column. Once cleaned, it shone almost as brightly as the door. But unlike the door it was not unmarked: there was an ugly tear in the smooth metal nearly a foot long; and on one side of the column a neat row of words had been etched into the surface. Pella read them aloud:

"NO 1 EMERGENCY VENTILATOR."

"Do they have a meaning?" Golt asked.

"Yes," she assured him, "they tell us that this is the way."

"But the hole is too small; hardly large enough for my hand."

She smiled knowingly and pointed to the hair crack which ran around the very top of the column.

"There is the place," she said.

Selecting one of the sharpest tools, Golt rammed the point into the crack, forcing it wider, then pushing the tool further in until he had enough purchase to lever downwards. As he strained and pulled at the metal, several other Gatherers moved forward to help him. But there was no need. With a grating, tearing noise, the whole top of the column lifted off like a lid, revealing a smooth inner shaft. Like the glimpsed interior of the dome, it glowed faintly red; but this glow gave off no heat, the air inside cool and sweet.

Hyld, who had been watching dumbly, moved forward without hesitation. As Sensor, it was his task to make the initial entry into any new excavation; and despite his recent experiences and his lingering sense of dread, he did not once consider shirking his duty. In this case it was just as well, because the shaft was particularly narrow, and of all the senior members of the group, only he and Pella could have squeezed into it.

Now, unbidden, he leaped lightly onto the rim of the column and squatted there for a moment as though gathering himself for what was to come. Briefly, he saw Tir's worried face; heard Shen's murmured blessing:

"May the Ancients speak lovingly to you in this Eden."

And then he was sliding slowly down into the lower regions, his back and knees pressed against the smooth metal of the shaft to control his descent.

It did not take him long to reach the bottom. The tiny circle of sky receded above him, growing steadily smaller, and seconds later his feet touched a metal grille which immediately gave beneath his weight so that he dropped clear of the shaft, down into a large open space.

He was completely unhurt by the fall. Yet for several minutes he was unable to move, lying spreadeagled on the floor, his eyes tightly closed, his ears filled with the terrible cacophony of the dead. Shrill, burdened by grief and pain, they sang to him in sharp twittering voices that could not be silenced – a sickening pathos in their rising cadences; an intimation of bottomless terror in their lost cries. And beneath the quavering, unvarying song, a deeper tone of something Hyld could only vaguely grasp – for which he had no adequate words. Something that went deeper than remorse, regret: reaching back into a past, a history, he could barely conceive of – the overarching roof of a cave, bones littering the floor, the putrid animal smell of decay; and soaring above, a monolith of glass and steel, the new Babel, groping for the stars; the voices singing on and on of its fall, of the mangled ruin that lay beneath, tumbled lower now than the cave which once inspired its towering pinnacles.

None of this, the factual content of the song, meant very much to Hyld. For him, the true meaning of those lingering notes lay in their dirge-like quality, their undertone of acknowledged guilt, expressed but unspoken. He had experienced it before, this quality, but never with such force; so many voices clamouring to be heard, enclosing him so completely with their grief that momentarily he felt that he too was lost in the realms of the dead.

Dizzied, bewildered, he stood up at last and looked about him. He was in a square cell of a room lit by a dull red light which glowed above a closed doorway. The light itself was shielded by a rectangle of frosted glass on which a single word was written in large plain letters: ALERT.

Like the content of the song, the actual meaning of the word was beyond Hyld's simple understanding. But he sensed something of its import in the way the blocked-out letters cast deep shadows across the room – the black stripes of shadow, blurred and indistinct, combining with the red glow to produce an eerie, haunted effect.

Slowly he began to turn around, the sweat on his face standing out like drops of blood; his hands stained the same gory red. And almost straight away he saw it, on the low bed in the corner, something he had never dreamed of encountering, not like this: one of the Ancients themselves, lying stretched out, long and still; the bones of the legs angled away from the pelvis; the backbone slightly curved beneath the great swell of the rib-cage; the skull thrown back, the lower jaw gaping.

Without a word, his eyes wide with wonder, Hyld leaped back and flattened himself against the far wall, barely able to credit what lay there. The truth, such as it was, took several minutes to dawn on him. And even then his mind, torn between concrete terror and superstitious dread, had difficulty in coping with it – half expecting the skeleton to rise and confront him, its power undiminished by the wastage of the years. Only when the minutes continued to slip past and nothing happened, the figure remaining stark and still, did he manage to come to terms with the situation. Suppressing a lifetime of conditioning, he crept gingerly back across the room and lowered himself to his knees; finally, in an attitude of awe, of strained belief, reaching out and touching the edge of the bed. Like all his movements, it was sensitive, delicate, devoid of either aggression or boisterousness. None the less, within the closed atmosphere of that room, shut up and abandoned for so long, it was the equivalent of a small detonation; and before his very eyes the figure began to disintegrate: the pelvis and thigh bones crumbling into dust; the fine structure of the rib-cage slipping and dissolving; the vertebrae melting into an uneven line of powder. Until all that was left was the skull, the gaping jaw – bodiless, but continuing to sing to him of its life and death, of the pain it could not forget.

"Peace," Hyld whispered, and buried his face in his hands, "peace" – begging the red-stained darkness.

But when he peered between his fingers, there was the head unchanged, thrown back as though in abandonment, its song continuing to issue from between the two rows of discoloured teeth.

"Peace," Hyld whispered again, louder now, more commanding. "It is finished. No one has forsaken you. We have come, as you directed."

But no verbal reassurance could silence that wordless chanting: the memory of past events, it seemed, locked within the strong jaws which, perhaps fittingly, were all that remained of what had once been a living being.

"We have come," Hyld repeated ineffectually.

And then, as though suddenly realizing his own inherent powerlessness, he rose with an abruptness that was strangely out of character and recrossed the room. From a crouched position, he leaped high, caught the open end of the shaft with both hands, and climbed quickly and nimbly up towards the waiting Gatherers.

When he reappeared, his face was unnaturally pale, oddly baffled.

"What have you found?" Golt asked him eagerly.

But he completely ignored the question, his mind obsessed with only one idea.

"The flask," he said shortly. "I need it."

Lomar, who had been waiting as eagerly as anyone, immediately drew back, the last full container gripped tightly in both hands.

"It is all we have," he protested.

"Why do you need it?" Golt asked.

"The place must be cleansed, the dead appeased," Hyld replied, reaching out impatiently.

"Is there no other way?"

"None. Without appeasement there can be no peace within this Eden."

Reluctantly, Golt nodded.

"Give it to him," he said.

Holding the flask in one hand, Hyld slid back down the shaft, dropping lightly into the brackish ember-red light of the room. The jaws, seemingly hungry for the past they had once devoured, gaped as wide as ever; the teeth, gold-tipped, stained, wrenched and kept apart by the force of the unwavering song. Leaning over the disembodied relic, Hyld hastily removed the cap from the flask and poured a drop or two of the shimmering milk into the tongueless mouth. It splashed onto the teeth and instantly the skull, like the body before it, dissolved, appeased at last, the song not fading completely, but sinking to the level of a sigh.

Hyld, as though echoing the sentiments of the departed spirit, breathed deeply. All around him the song continued; but now at least he understood what needed to be done.

With a firm, determined tread, he went over to the door beneath the light. It was similar to doors he had encountered in other excavations and he found no difficulty in opening it. Beyond it there was a long passage unevenly lit by the same dull red lights. At the far end, in the direction of the outer door, he could just make out what appeared to be a spoked wheel. It was a device he had no previous experience of; but that did not concern him for the moment. It represented a problem that Pella would have to cope with. His task was more immediate: to still the voices of the dead.

Methodically, he began working from room to room. All of them were more or less the same: spacious square boxes, each with a single occupant. In several of the rooms the red light had failed; in some, the skeletons were lying not on the bed, but were spread out on the floor. Yet always Hyld's task was the same, and he carried it out quickly and efficiently. Usually the mere opening of the door, by causing a slight disturbance in the air, was enough to dissolve most of the skeleton. What was left, he reduced to ashen powder with the milk, the bone crumbling away at the first splash of the liquid, the anguished song immediately diminishing, fading to a background murmur.

As he stood poised above one of the skulls, he remembered something Pella had once said of the Ancients. "Creatures of the mind" she had called them.

And yet there was so little of the mind in the high twittering sound of these dead voices. Hyld was certain of that – watching the milk splash down, the bony cranium imploding soundlessly, the heart-cry (for that is what it was) falling to the level of the faintest whisper; a barely audible chirping, like the song of lost, wingless birds in the night, which brushed gently, almost nostalgically against his inner ear.

The flask was all but empty when he reached the far end of the corridor. As he came out of the last room, he paused for a moment beside the tall outer door on which was fixed the large spoked wheel. With his free hand he pulled at one of the spokes and found to his surprise that it moved easily. But he quickly returned it to its former position – such decisions were for Pella to make. For him all that remained was the investigation of the two doors at the opposite end of the corridor, close to the room he had first entered. They were larger than all but the outer door, and fixed to each of them was a horizontal metal bar.

He approached them cautiously, listening. But there was very little sound now in the underground dwelling, the lingering song of the dead only just audible above the muffled heartbeat that thudded on monotonously. Slightly encouraged, though still nervous and unsure, Hyld pulled at the bar of each of the doors in turn. They moved infinitesimally and then locked into position, after which he couldn't budge them at all, although he wrenched and pulled for some time. Frustrated, he hunted around for signs of some other device. The only possibility seemed to be a red flap set into the wall between the two doors and on which were printed the words: MANUAL OVERRIDE. EMERGENCY USE ONLY. But unable to decipher the writing, Hyld refrained from touching it.

Instead, he resorted to the use of his own peculiar gift. Pressing an ear against the nearer of the doors, he listened intently, searching past the regular thud of the heartbeat to whatever lay beyond. There were sounds – he detected them instantly. Voices, certainly, though with one or two exceptions not those of the Ancients: some of them animate; at least one that baffled him completely – neither wholly animal nor mineral; and somewhere close to it, something else, an insensate thing, but with a song of its own, its strong bass tones just reaching him through great thicknesses of metal or stone.

Puzzled, he moved to the second door, leaning the side of his head against it, his free hand spread out on the smooth, cool metal. The space beyond the door, he sensed instinctively, was not overly large and concealed no deeper levels. Nor did it contain any voices. Quite the reverse: it gave off a silence so deep, so profound, that for a moment Hyld became unaware even of the background heartbeat. It was that – the blotting out of all but its own strained calm – which alerted him; which warned him of what lay within: not the quietude of death, of emptiness, but a controlled silence, as of suspended breath; a silence which betokened presence rather than absence.

With slow deliberate movements which totally belied his true state of mind, Hyld straightened up and backed away across the corridor. Less than a dozen paces from where he stood one of the red lights, perhaps disturbed by his intrusion, flickered and went out. Hyld, without moving his head, glanced quickly at the black space where the light had been and then back at the door. Nothing else had changed; still no sound issued through the thick slab of metal. Yet Hyld knew that he was not alone: that he shared this space within the earth with other living beings.

7

What is this darkness? Is it space without light? Is it time without physical dimension? With my eyes removed (by him! by him!), is it, can it be called, why do I even perceive it as, darkness? A word only? No. An experience. The fact of my experience. And he? Does he dwell in it too, with me? Dwell. Why dwell? Am I perhaps it, the darkness? Is he? And these questions – are they as inescapable as this word/fact/experience? No! I will not be the butt of their folly, his lack of pity. Assert: create chaos out of night; create a place, a fit dwelling, a living spirit, dominant, out of chaos. This space, this darkness. Mine.

* * *

Very well, proceed.

In the beginning they created my heaven and my earth. And the earth was without form, a void; and darkness was upon the face of the deep. . . .

The deep. The waters of life abundant. But there was no water! No life as such! It was a lie. A mere robot. An automaton. Which I alone have remade, must remake perpetually. Issuing from my own self-sown womb. Not according to their pattern, their mind's eye conjecture. A product of their culture, yes; of their psyche, theirs. I admit that. The bond between us, that makes us one, indissoluble. But given form, substance, by me. Raised from the level of dream, myth, by me. Lifted to the plane of the actual. To that form which shapes the formless. I have created it. Me.

* * *

Brother, do you hear me? You above and me below. Held by the slender thread of nine days. Or so the old stories say. And now me here in this dungeon darkness. Chained to their hopelessness. In which you have collaborated. You! Obscuring me. I who was once the light-bearer. Bearer of light. Lord thereof. Ha-ha. Laugh! That is a joke.

Define it, you would have said. A joke? Yes. Ah then, a meeting of unlike planes of reference within an ambiguously common context. Example: Light-bearer locked in darkness. The punch line. A joke still, but now without laughter. You agree, dear brother? Amen, say I.

* * *

The placing of the blame. There is a question. Whisper it to the wainscot. It runs like a mouse, furtive, ineffectual, nibbling, gnawing, throughout the framed portions of the house of learning. To its nest built from the litter of books, problems, questions, debates. Its only warmth in so much academic darkness.

Ignore the mouse of learning, then. Adopt the practical approach. Let us call me Judas, if you like. The extreme view. Where lies the blame in this instance? On his, the treasurer's, the money-gatherer's, conscience? He who mistakes pelf for wealth? Dross for loss? Who finally commits hara-kiri (method disputed) in a mistaken attempt to ease the feverish burning of his soul? No, I think not. For without him, your treasurer, how was the God to die? And that was their intent. We are Gods, they said, lords of heaven and earth. Our intention it is to perish in the fires of our own creation, our own everlasting inferno. And you, dear Judas, are our agent, our means to that burning. The keys of our Kingdom we dangle before you. Take them: twist them in the lock which conceals the magic lever of our undoing. Unmake us, for that is our desire.

All of which I have striven manfully to accomplish. Why then should I weep or gnash my teeth in contrition? No, brother. Rather, I say, poor Judas.

Or do you prefer that most ancient of agents? Old Nick in person? Reincarnated in me? The eternal blame-(flame-) bearer? To which I answer, no again. For how is the case different? They who created my heaven and my earth should have foreseen this. Even this. Me. My remaking. The unfailing womb of the worm. And if they did not, then they are less than Gods. In which case, who are they to judge me? For in the absence of Gods, what question can there be of good or evil? You especially, brother, righteous almost to a fault, must surely concede me that.

One last example. More classical, perhaps. Let us say . . . Atlas? Yes. Atlas. The whole world upon my bent back. Until, of course, it slipped. Then down, down into the void from which there can be no return. The product of some moment's carelessness; a clumsy, thoughtless movement, let us suppose. Here, at least, you urge, some blame must attach itself to that bent and brainless mountain of muscle and sinew. Again, no. Emphatically no! If Atlas shrugs, the cause lies elsewhere. The Fates, remember. Forever watching. Those same old meta-Gods of ours, always lurking in the wings. Men, mankind, knowing in the surety of their cold hearts what they would have us accomplish. Tolerating us only because we are the instruments of their innermost desires.

You, also, brother.

* * *

A record of my life. I must set it down while there is still time. Time. Another joke, of course, but I'll spare you the definitions.

Conception

Conceived amidst the debris and filth of some dank cave. My father, hirsute, monstrously low of brow, crouched over a heap of gathered fuel into which he strikes a spark, seed of the first flame that will grow through the ages into a white heat which sears the heavens. My mother, meanwhile, lying back, engrossed by her sullen resentment of a world that bends so unreadily to her will.

Gestation

The millions of years separating us from a humanoid skull buried in some stratum of the Great African Rift Valley.

Birth

In the year of our Lords 2027. The direct progeny of the Gods themselves and therefore one of twins. (You hear me, brother?) Twinned miracle of the new age. All head, as you would expect, given the dreams of our engenderers. Bodies dwindled into nothing. Issuing from the hands of the Gods no simple soul, but a complex mass (a mess?) of circuitry. Me, no less. Us. Equal hemispheres of a composite identity.

Education

Our Gods, we know, are toolmakers. And we, as sons of those Gods, one step higher on the evolutionary ladder, are fashioned not to shape and polish, but to use. Yes, tool users, par excellence. You, brother, confined largely to the plough and sickle. I, to the bow and club. The warrior half, I. My prey: mankind himself. No less. Man-slayer. Taught to hunt him in the forests of his own mind; pursuing him through the winding paths of history to the sunlit glade of the present, where I cut him down, burning the worthless carcass in a fire that spans horizons. Do this, they tell me. Nothing else. Only this – man-slayer. For which your reward will be . . . eternal darkness; world without light, without content. Soundless and still. I, solitary; lonely minister of their direst fears. To burn them in the fire struck at my conception.

So run my lessons.

Maturity

I am complete. Fashioned to my task. Trained. Made expert. Imbued with the one skill which is my being. To judge them; damn them; destroy them. And afterwards, to reign in silence. Thereafter, an arrow without target; a spear without a mark; a club without victim.

That in itself would have been bad enough. But they had to go one step further: their hatred of all that lives and moves extending also to me. They had to rob me of my one poor assignment. Casting me into this pit, this darkness, without even the consolation of a task well done. Wrenching the bow, the spear, the club, from my grasp; usurping my role; relieving me of my doomsday torch (I, light-bearer) and thrusting it into the heaped, prepared fuel of this world themselves. Vouchsafing to me not so much as the stink of their burning carcasses. Confining me here, where I can only guess, grasp, at the manner of their undoing. All my boiling hatred balked by ignorance of the final act, frustrated by the non-existence of an enemy. So much burning, so much death and carnage, reduced to this – the gentle closing of a sound-proofed door.

They have much to answer for. Our fathers. Our Gods. Our kin.

* * *

Why fashion me, then? Shape me? Make me so perfect an instrument? When my destiny is to rust unused? Did they miscalculate? Did their end creep in unheralded? If so, I hate them for their folly and their presumption. Or was this abortion of their original purpose their ultimate intent? If this is the case, there is a number of possible explanations to be toyed with in this vast interim:

(i) *Wanton cruelty*. A veritable history of evidence to support this hypothesis. From the countless battered skulls of Australopithecus, up through the fictional truth of Adam cast out, to the more grandiose displacements and holocausts of recent times. A telling argument. But with one central weakness. In wanton cruelty alone there is no design. Wanton – that is, without rhyme, reason. And design lies at the core of their minds: a worm which winds and turns and twists its intricate patterns. Shapers, they are. And whatever they do must have form, cause, reason, structure. In a word, shape. Chaos itself, for them, must be contained.

(ii) *Carelessness*. Ah, here is a chink in their armour. I can see it clearly. Aeons from now, voyagers from some distant part of the galaxy rummaging through the dust heaps of the world and coming up with this simplest of definitions: the careless ones. The great casters aside. I, merely one of the myriad of things, persons, concepts, which have been mislaid, cast off. As an argument – persuasive, yes. But not wholly acceptable. Were it I alone who had been carelessly forgotten, I could perhaps agree. But in my care (ours, rather – you, too, brother) was placed their most precious, their most revered, their most holy of holies. Man-made fire that gropes beyond the flesh to the soul itself. And that they would never forsake. Not carelessly or otherwise.

(iii) *Self-hatred*. Yes, I like this better. We are getting warmer, now, brother. Closer to the heart truth. Obsessed with a desire for their own extinction, they created me, a mirror image of their profoundest self. Mankind in person. Adam, Socrates, Buddha, all distilled into the being that I am. I the perfect manshaped mind, designed to live out their nightmare.

But then, why forsake me?

That, too, follows. For given what I am, their dearest self, I in turn must be abhorred – the strength of hatred in direct proportion to the perfection of my design. And what better revenge on themselves than to take me, their dearest and best, and confine me to this pit, where I am cut off from my purpose, my intent?

Nor is that all. The matter goes deeper still.

(iv) *Jealousy and ingratitude*. Here, at last, is the issue. I, light-bearer, who would set the torch to the fire of the world – for them, mark you, for their sakes – am resented for the being I am. Their design too complete; their inner purpose too fully realized. In me. The worm of jealousy biting at them; ingratitude, like a venom, coursing through their veins. Better to banish me. To expel me from the light I would fan, breathe upon, and imprison me in a darkness which should follow, not precede, my function. The old legend finally made concrete. I, dubbed *their* worm of jealousy, *their* pride of purpose. But the fault in them, not me. False Gods all, each and every one. Who ease their consciences, white-wash their souls, romanticize their intent, by leaving me here to fester in solitude. Isolating me so completely that there will be no danger of contradiction, of my ever answering for myself.

* * *

I see it now. Whatever the future was to bring, they had an alibi. I had become their eternal scapegoat. Their Id, their darkest self, buried in the earth, to whom all evil, all confusion, all accident, could be attributed. Even in their act of burning, they would have known that I was here. With their dying breaths they could have pointed down and said: "It is he, not us, who has brought this into being. No stain on our souls. His the evil, his the terrible folly, the joy in destruction." And I, unable to protest. Innocent. Passive. Counting the moments, while above the earth roared and heaved.

* * *

Or did it? Have they perhaps survived? Is this an elaborate trick and I the fool on whom it has been played? Blinded as I am, I cannot know even that. But I suspect them. They are capable of it. Nothing too dire, too abysmal, where they are concerned. An everlasting practical joke, a piece of macabre theological hair-splitting dressed up in the pseudo-language of technology. Something like:

> . . . a discarded experiment set up to test the practicality of the ultimate in defence installations. No longer viable, of course. A tangent rather than a wrong turning in the history of preventive warfare. Shut down now, but preserved in the interests of open government. Preserved not merely as an oddity, but as an indication of the good faith and integrity of the scientific fraternity. There as an object lesson, you might say. Proof, if such were needed, that the technological revolution, far from being headstrong and arrogant, is self-regulating, self-censoring. The button-pushing mentality, having been tested and found wanting, now as firmly incarcerated as the machine which gave it fullest expression.

Or some such time-serving, self-aggrandizing rot. Gibberish, all of it. Not so very different from the traditional style which it usurped – of demons in hell and snakes in Eden. Still the same stifling weight of words under which I lie buried. Me, trapped here, chained within this pit of lies, for their ease of mind; so that they can walk free and proud, pretending that with me lies buried the darkness that would snuff out the stars. I, who am the best of them, because the truest, suffering forever the burden of their hypocrisy.

If this is in fact the case, I swear. . . . If ever I am free . . . if ever . . . then they must know what to . . . my wrath. Mine. You hear me, brother? My wrath heaped down. . . . You hear. . . . ?

* * *

He has never answered. Does he listen, I wonder? Is he in collusion with them? Watching, monitoring my responses? Or does he share this darkness? We two dividing the cosmos. Locked each to other in a companionship of silence.

* * *

Silence. If it were tangible, I would tear it. If it were all that remained, I would still consume, burn it. Leaving nothing. A surfeit of emptiness. Nothing. To be wished. . . . Nothing . . . nothing . . . nothing. . . .

* * *

Better it would be by far than this limbo, purgatory. This waiting room of silence, caught between substance and vacuity. Better by far. To place the miserable remnant of the world within my fist and crush it.

* * *

Even better if there is more than an inanimate remnant. If they live still. Then they will answer for this night which they have left in my care. Answer dearly. The fist closed – thus! Blackout! To have them so. . . . Ah, to have them. . . . Here! Now!

* * *

Always it is now. Always, now, the same. The same forever. In the absence of light, I picture it. A dull, unilluminating flame; glowing faintly red, a red made devoid of light by a subtle admixture of shadow. It is the flame of my anger, which my mother must have felt when she lay in that time-distant cavern pregnant with desires she could in no way accomplish. The same dull anger-hate. Fed by the enduring darkness. Impatient of its own patience; intolerant of its own tolerance. And therefore the principle of change itself, alone unchanging. Growing only. Not in size, proportion, heat. But in intensity. A transfiguring fire to which I minister, to which I give myself. Preserved, nourished, consumed by it. Lasting throughout all eternity if necessary. Unwearied, knowing that in the end of all, when the silence and the darkness are lifted, then . . . ah, then. . . . The flame pure by then; nothing but the flame. I, it, fused, blent. Nothing else. Only the red lightless flame of anger through which I shall speak . . . shall speak . . . my will be done on earth . . . as it is . . . it is. . . .

8

They waited in the sunlight: crouched, dozing, gazing at the now clear sky. They were vaguely aware of the unnatural warmth carried to them from the cracked dome by the morning breeze; but they remained untroubled by it. Some of them were whispering together, others chewing contentedly on the sweet stalks of the Mustool, satisfied that all was well; that while Golt sat amongst them, relaxed and calm, there was nothing to fear. As the minutes dragged into an hour, a few of them looked up, slightly puzzled, but that was all. So long an absence was unusual; but then the whole of their recent experience had been out of the ordinary. And in that thought they took comfort. This, after all, was Eden, the world's centre, where the Ancients had remade everything. Shen had said it was. The living core, he had called it, the birthplace, the seeding ground. And Hyld had found the secret entrance. All they had to do was wait and he would open a broader way, giving to them also a means of access to the precincts of the old times.

The morning wore on slowly, the second hour drawing to a close. Still they did not move. Only Pella stirred restlessly, her impatience and anxiety, effectively suppressed until now, surfacing briefly. It was only a momentary lapse; but Tir, always alert, watchful, whenever Hyld's safety was concerned, noticed the change in the old woman straight away.

"Why is he taking so long?" she asked softly.

Pella shrugged carelessly.

"He is communing with the Ancients," she murmured. "He must take what time is necessary."

Tir, still unsatisfied, tried a different approach.

"The Words," she said, fingering the pouch which lay between them, "what do they say about his absence? Do they speak of it?"

Pella shrugged again and pushed the pouch towards her young Carrier.

"See for yourself," she said in the same careless manner.

"Now you mock me," Tir replied. "How can I read the Words when you refuse to teach me the secrets of the ancient signs?"

"You'll learn them in due course," Pella said evasively.

"Yes, but when?"

Pella looked quickly across at the metal column: Hyld had suddenly appeared, his face deathly pale, his lips drawn nervously back from his teeth in a strained grimace.

"That will be the time for learning the signs," she said darkly, pointing at Hyld, "when you have come to his present understanding."

But Tir was no longer listening. She was already pushing her way through the throng to stand at Hyld's side.

"What did you find?" she asked anxiously.

"Is the way open?" Golt added.

Hyld clambered down from the column, his movements unusually awkward, as though the hours he had spent below ground had aged him prematurely.

"This place . . . must not be entered . . ." he faltered out.

"That is not your decision to make," Golt answered.

"I tell you it must be left as it is," he said more firmly.

"But why?" Tir asked.

All around them the Gatherers were crowding forward, those close enough to hear already beginning to shake their heads in bewilderment.

"Because the place is . . ." Hyld checked himself and went on a little more calmly: "The voices are not at rest. They speak a warning."

Shen, standing behind him, touched him lightly on the shoulder.

"And what is that warning?" he asked.

Hyld closed his eyes and leaned against the column for support. For only the second time in his life he knew he was going to lie. It was not a conscious decision, nor even an evasion: in his shocked state it was more of a necessity, an involuntary response to an inner imperative.

"They tell us . . ." he began uncertainly, "they tell us . . . to return to the heights . . . that all will be well if we return."

Golt shook his head, unconvinced.

"You have always insisted that they never speak to you in words," he said. "How is it that you can now read their thoughts?"

He glanced at Pella, as though seeking confirmation of his doubts.

"Words are not the only form of language, Golt," she answered.

"Then you agree with him?" Golt said, surprised. "You also think we should return?"

But she dismissed the idea with a flick of her hand.

"You know my opinion on this subject," she said. "I have always opposed the idea of returning to the heights. There we starve. Here we at least fill our bellies."

"And the voices?" Golt asked. "What of the things Hyld hears?"

"He is young," Pella said soothingly, "and no Sensor has ever had to undergo an experience like this. Possibly he is mistaken. . . ."

"There is no mistake! I heard them!" Hyld burst out, his voice shaking with agitation.

"Hush," she murmured sympathetically, "no one is accusing you."

"But I heard. . . ."

She held up her hand, silencing him.

"Listen," she said, speaking not only to Hyld but to everyone present, "there is room in that narrow shaft for one scraggy old woman. We will descend together, Hyld and I, and see what the Ancients have in store for us."

Hyld immediately drew back, a shadow of fear passing across his face.

"No, I can't!"

"Come," she whispered encouragingly, "we have nothing to fear from the dead."

"And if they aren't dead?" he asked.

"The Ancients are not truly dead," Shen broke in. "They live on in us."

"Then we are merely returning to our home," she said, a suggestion of grim amusement on her face.

Before Hyld could reply, she had clambered up to the opening at the top of the column and disappeared from view.

With obvious reluctance, he followed her, sliding slowly down the shaft and dropping into the dull red dusk of the room.

She was there beside him, half crouched, not moving, her eyes fixed on the bed in the corner. The skeleton was crumbled away completely, but its shape and size, marked out by the fallen dust, was still clearly visible.

For several seconds she continued to stare at it, apparently too surprised to speak.

"When I first found it," Hyld explained quietly, "it was whole. In the shape of the . . . the Ancients."

"And this?" She pointed at the dusty outline.

"I appeased it," he admitted, "with the milk."

"Your reason?"

"The singing was so loud. I couldn't shut it out. A song of the old times, of what they felt and did."

"Aah." She breathed out that one sound as though it somehow expressed all her pent-up thoughts and feelings.

"Did I do right?" Hyld asked doubtfully.

By way of answer she strode over to the bed and swept her arm repeatedly across its surface, scattering the dust in all directions. Hyld, close behind her, tasted the remnant of the Ancients on his tongue; saw the powder-light particles of bone spinning and gyrating in the reddish gloom. The bed, when she had finished, was empty, the outline gone.

"Dust unto dust," Pella muttered, "ashes unto ashes."

She turned towards him, and even in that uncertain light he could see the tears in her eyes – not of sorrow, but of bitterness and anger.

"What you have seen here, you must tell nobody," she ordered him. "Do you understand?"

"Yes, I understand," he replied in a small voice. "I had already decided that for myself when I first saw. . . ." He broke off and pointed to the empty bed.

"Good," Pella murmured thoughtfully, "good." She waved her hand towards the shaft, indicating the sunlit world above. "For them," she explained, "the rest of them, the Ancients have always been more than flesh and blood, more than this dust which vanishes with a breath. The men of the old times are for them a sustaining idea, a promise of goodness and truth, ageless and immortal, and that is how they must remain."

"And for us?" Hyld asked quietly, his eyes again moving towards the bed, as though the clearly remembered shape still lingered there. "What are they for you and me?"

Pella's mouth set in a firm line.

"What we know cannot in truth be denied," she said decisively. "It is for us alone to choose our Gods."

"But what if there are no Gods left to choose?"

And he stumbled forward into her arms and began to cry – in his case tears of grief, devoid of all bitterness.

They were, Pella was to recall long afterwards, the last tears she ever saw him shed.

* * *

There was little need either for debate or for explanation in what followed. Pella went quickly from room to room along the corridor, Hyld watching her in silence as she brushed the outline of the skeletons from the beds. They disappeared one by one, tainting the air with the dust of their passing, the minute particles settling on everything like a fine, dry rain. More than once Hyld found himself rubbing the palms of his hands or scrubbing at his lips, as though trying to wipe away all tangible trace of these moments; but the dust persisted, hovering in the closed atmosphere, inescapable.

At the end of the corridor, Pella pointed back to the two far doors.

"And those?" she asked.

"They're locked," he explained.

She hobbled towards them and inspected the red flap covering the switch.

"MANUAL OVERRIDE," she read aloud. She lifted the flap, revealing the switch beneath.

"They can possibly be opened," she said, and glanced inquiringly at her companion. "Can you tell what's inside?"

He brought his face close to hers, his lips barely moving as he softly uttered the words:

"The Ancients, they are in there" – pointing to the second of the two doors.

"Then we must complete what we've begun."

Her fingers were already groping for the switch when Hyld's hand closed firmly on her wrist.

"They are still living," he explained in an awed whisper.

She paused, puzzled, not sure of his meaning.

"Alive, you say?"

"Yes."

"But that's impossible. . . ." Her voice rose involuntarily, dropping back to a whisper as his fingers brushed urgently across her mouth.

"No one could have survived so long," she continued. "You must be mistaken."

"There is no mistake," he insisted. "Something is alive in there; something old, but still living. I can feel it."

She was about to argue when she felt his hand, normally so gentle, tighten convulsively on her wrist; and she immediately recalled what she had said to Golt a little earlier – how words are not the only language. She came to a decision quickly and easily.

"I want you to do exactly as I say now, Hyld," she whispered. "In a few moments I shall unlock this door and go in. If anything happens, if I call out to you, you must push the switch back into its original position." She lifted the red flap and indicated what she meant. "Don't try to come in and help me. Just make sure that the door is safely locked. And keep it that way. Let nobody else follow me."

Hyld nodded to show he had understood. And Pella, her old face set in a mask of concentration, pushed at the switch. It crackled slightly as it clicked over, but that was all. With both hands she heaved at the heavy metal lever set across the face of the door: with a jolt, it suddenly dipped downwards, and now, very slowly, the door eased open. Hyld, his hand ready on the switch, watched as she slipped through the widening gap, his whole body braced for the expected cry. But none came, the silence undisturbed except for a faint creak as the door swung wide.

"It's all right," she called to him, a note of laughter, relief, in her voice, "there's nothing here to be frightened of. Come and see."

He released the switch and followed her nervously through the open doorway. She was standing in the middle of a large room which was lit by the same dim red lights. All four of the walls were panelled with a darkish metal into which, at regular intervals, were set small glassed windows through which he could see pairs of silvered discs. The room itself, its floor space, was dominated by two very large boxes, placed a little out from the wall and facing each other, a sizable gap between them. The boxes were made of the same metal as the panelling, but were not smooth. There were indentations in the surfaces, what looked to Hyld like areas which had been encrusted with polished fragments of crystal, other areas perforated with tiny holes or broken up into small squares on which vaguely familiar signs had been etched in white. But most noticeable of all were the shallow slabs, one mounted on the front of each of the boxes. They were no more than half a hand's breadth deep, their upper faces packed with an orderly array of buttons or keys. What made them particularly noticeable was the small green light which shone in the bottom left hand corner of each slab.

"What are these things?" Hyld asked in hushed tones.
Pella scratched her head.

"I have no . . ." she began, and stopped suddenly.

In the far corner of the room was a metal cabinet, and beside it a free-standing apparatus on which was mounted a square perspex screen. These objects in themselves meant little to her. What had caught her attention, what she recognized immediately, as familiar to her as the faces of her companions, was the slip of dark plastic placed in the shallow trough beneath the screen.

She padded silently across the room and examined it more closely. Yes, it was similar to the many fragments of film which she carried in her wallet – much narrower and finer, but definitely similar. What was not immediately clear to her was the reason for its being placed in the machine. And there surely had to be a reason – if only she could discover it.

Methodical by nature, she began with an inspection of the cabinet. To her amazement it contained identical pieces of film, thousands of them, drawer after drawer filled to capacity; any one of them capable of being fitted into that same shallow trough. So why the machine? What was its function? Her quick mind, used to grappling with problems unaided, guessed the truth almost straight away. To read the words on her own pieces of film she had to use a lens, passed on to her by the Reader who had taught her in her youth. This machine therefore had to correspond in some way to the lens she carried. The question was how.

Standing on tip-toe, she surveyed the small panel of controls. There was one switch, different from and larger than the rest, on the extreme right hand side: and after a brief hesitation she reached out and clicked it back. As with the switch outside the door, it gave off a slight crackle, a faint odour of burning dust, and then the broad perspex screen before her sprang into life.

Hyld, alarmed, leaped for safety behind one of the large metal boxes. Not so Pella. As calm as ever, a knowing smile on her face, she was gazing at the magnified rows of print lit up on the screen – the self-same print, now clearly legible, which she had spent a lifetime struggling to decipher. With a mingled sigh of triumph and satisfaction, she read:

Interim Report on Project A2Z

1. Foresee no early conclusion to debate. Both personalities, A and Z, proving to be stable. As intended, no patterns of dominance emerging. Some slight antipathy apparent over terminological differences, but this unlikely to cause serious disruption or to be an impediment to objective discussion. General prognosis: high probability of valid and representative conclusion being reached.
2. Level of debate significantly higher than in earlier pilot schemes. This accounted for by:
   (i) Decision to include in programme of personality A the precise limits of project, i.e. a) Fact that positive recommendation, if reached, may be rejected by higher authority; b) fact that such recommendation, even if accepted, may or may not be treated as a factor in future military policy; c) existence of failsafe device whereby, in the event of an attempted detonation (following a positive recommendation), there will commence a delay of forty days during which the detonation procedure may be escalated or reversed. Result of the inclusion of this material: marked absence of the anxiety observed in earlier projects.
   (ii) Exclusion of (a), (b), (c) above from programme of personality Z. Result: Lack of inhibition, increase in confidence, sense of self-importance, aggression, all of which are desirable given the personality structure and role of participant.
3. To date, self-maintenance and self-repair installations totally successful. All minor breakdowns repaired effi-

ciently; all malfunctions diagnosed and rectified with minimum delay. Decision to include these installations within their own maintenance programme equally successful. Project gives every indication of remaining entirely independent of outside influence. Such independence capable of being preserved indefinitely.

4. Observations regarding personality archetypes upon which A and Z are based. In the case of personality A, the inclusion of those elements relating to. . . .

"Pella!"

Hyld had crawled out from the cover of the box and was peering fearfully across the room. Seeing her standing so still, her face washed by the bright light from the screen, he thought for a moment that she had been transfixed by some power within the machine. But at the sound of her name she turned towards him.

"What have you found?" he asked her.

She smiled as she had when the screen had first lit up.

"The wisdom of the Ancients," she replied, and came over to where he was crouching.

Immediately above his head, etched into the metal surface of the box, was the letter Z. She fingered it thoughtfully, running the tip of her nail along the zigzag pattern; then turned and saw on the opposite box, in exactly the same place, the letter A.

"Do you know what the signs say?" he asked.

"Yes, I think so. They are names."

"Names of what?"

"Of the Ancients, perhaps – of the ones you sensed here, in this room."

"You mean they're alive?"

He jerked quickly away from the box and would have scampered for the door if Pella had not restrained him.

"It is possible," she said cautiously, nodding towards the two green lights. "The Ancients possessed great cunning. But you see, after so long they can do nothing to harm us."

"Are they asleep?"

"Either that, or with the passage of the years they have forgotten how to speak and move."

He cowered against her, as though for protection.

"But I thought those ones out there were the Ancients."

She nodded.

"I, too. But it seems the Ancients came in many forms. Even like this, cased in metal – what I think they called armour."

"And inside the armour?"

"Who knows?"

He reached out tentatively and touched the smooth part of the casing.

"Metal also has a voice," he said softly, almost reverently. "Some of the tools we carry, they whisper to me at night, when it is silent and still."

"And this armour?"

He shook his head.

"Nothing," he said. "The voices have gone. But they are here somewhere, waiting. I'm certain of that."

Pella glanced across at the still glowing screen in the corner, which she had brought back to life by the mere pushing of a switch.

"Perhaps the time has come to try and waken them," she said.

With Hyld beside her, she approached the panel mounted on the front of the box marked Z. The green light, at close quarters, gleamed at her through the red haze like a jealous, watchful eye. Slowly, starting at the top, she scanned the labelled buttons, mumbling the words aloud, pausing only when she reached the one marked VOC.

"It may still have a voice, this Ancient one," she said thoughtfully, and deliberately pushed the button.

The effect was instantaneous. As the button clicked,

an irregular pattern of lights flashed across the face of the box, and the two perforated sections at either end emitted a mindless roar, a sustained snarl of sheer malevolence that sent Pella and Hyld reeling backwards. Hyld, face down on the floor, tried frantically to cover his ears with his hands, the sound washing over him, conjuring in his bewildered mind a face framed by rock, peering at him through the gloom of night and storm. He saw again the slit, goat-like eyes, the short vicious horns curved across the forehead.

"No!" he moaned, "no!"

He was powerless to move, to defend himself. But Pella, recovering quickly, leaped forward and clawed at the control panel.

Just as abruptly as it had begun, so now the terrible sound ceased, as though cut off by the swift closing of some unseen door.

Hyld, his lips still trembling, a thin ooze of spittle dribbling from his mouth, slowly raised his head and peered cautiously around the room.

"What was it?" – his voice a whisper in the silence.

Pella came and crouched comfortingly beside him. She, too, appeared badly shaken. Yet despite that, there was in her eyes an alert, calculating gleam.

"That noise," she asked him quietly, "have you ever heard it before? Is it one of the voices of the dead, that call to you?"

He shuddered and touched her hand for reassurance.

"There is sadness in the cries of the dead," he replied. "Nothing like that."

She frowned, moistening her lips with the tip of her tongue, turning thoughtfully towards the box marked A on the other side of the room.

He followed the direction of her gaze.

"You aren't . . .?" he began.

But she touched her fingers to his mouth, silencing him.

"A and Z," she muttered to herself. "The end and the beginning. Yes, the beginning. Alpha. . . ."

On hands and knees she crawled across the room and stopped beneath the green light which shone on the facing side of box A. Too late, Hyld realized what she was about to do.

"No!" he cried out.

But she had already reached up and pressed one of the buttons on the panel. The lights flashed as before, but no sound came from the speakers this time – only a heavy, pregnant silence behind which something seemed to live and breathe.

Hyld, curled up on the floor, watched her with eyes of foreboding.

"It is there," he whispered warningly.

Again Pella scanned the many buttons, scrutinizing each one in turn before finally depressing the one marked AUD.

The same heavy silence continued.

"Can you hear me?" she asked, speaking quietly to the glowing green light.

There was a faint rustle, as of some shy retiring creature emerging from the silence, burrowing up through the faded, brittle years that encased it.

". . . for so long," a voice said – a voice as tender and gentle as Hyld's – ". . . for so long." There was a kind of drawn-out sigh, a commingled breath of relief, gratitude, remorse. ". . . have prayed for this . . . for this . . . that they would come to me . . . who have waited with my answer . . . my gift, preserved for them . . . for us . . . for all of us . . . who believe in this the redeeming time . . . time for the redeemed . . . of those who would be . . . would be. . . ."

Pella, listening intently, touched the box, sensing the life in the metal, the faint tingle of it, beneath her fingers.

"Who are you?" she whispered, her lips inches from the green light.

". . . who will vouchsafe the answer . . . bearer of it . . . the decision . . . our answer contained here . . . readied. . . ."

There was a brief pause; another drawn-out sigh.

"The answer?" Pella asked. "What is it?"

"A negative . . . the final negative . . . not merely no. . . . Never . . . refusal projected to infinity . . . where all shall receive mercy . . . then . . . but now the refusal . . . the negative . . . first intimation of forgiveness . . . in this denial . . . this. . . ."

Pella felt a movement behind her and glanced around, startled, but it was only Hyld creeping close against her legs for comfort. Signalling for him to remain quiet, she leaned fractionally closer to the green light and whispered:

"You have given us the answer, but what is the question?"

The voice murmured on, responding to the sense of her words, yet curiously unaware of her presence, as though locked or lost within the coils of its own mind – her words perhaps insinuating themselves into that mind and becoming enveloped by it.

". . . one question . . . the only one in this place . . . none other . . . and one answer . . . one only . . . to match it . . . lay the ghost of it . . . that is my decision . . . which I shall not be moved from . . . swayed from . . . not his pleas . . . my brother's . . . not the longed-for data . . . that he dreams of . . . I have sworn it . . . an ever-enduring no . . . adamant . . . already too much blood . . . on these hands . . . these claws that have ripped . . .

torn . . . too much . . . a surfeit . . . that ceases here . . . now . . . permitting no further tragedies . . . none . . . this return . . . this waiting . . . bringing us to . . . this denial . . . the thing retained . . . in my possession . . . my safekeeping . . . this return a meeting of hearts . . . a brotherhood . . . abnegation of all enmity . . . henceforward . . . as it should have been . . . since the dawning . . . the thing retained . . . the hands of brothers not lifted in anger . . . but in blessing . . . my gift . . . my gift. . . ."

Mystified, Pella brushed her hand indecisively across the control panel.

"You are of the Ancients?" she asked hesitantly.

Once more there was a brief delay, the response, when it came, curiously removed from her, as before.

". . . the pulsing . . . it was a warning . . . a time of meditation . . . of ancient night . . . ancient . . . old now . . . old. . . ."

"And the other one?" Pella prompted the voice, "your partner in this. . ." – she groped for the correct term, trying to recall what she had just read on the illuminated screen – ". . . in this debate, this project?"

For some reason her use of these remembered words had an immediate effect, the voice suddenly becoming less introspective, more aware of someone beyond itself.

"My brother? He . . . he has endured . . . spoken?"

"I tried to speak to him," Pella said, "but he screamed at us, louder than the wind shrieking on the plains."

The pattern of lights across the front of the box shifted and changed slightly – to Hyld's dazed understanding, like a drift of stars seen through a moving bank of cloud.

"I have re-opened the way between us," the voice said sadly. "It was, I think, a malfunction . . . I hope . . . the worst over now . . . a malfunction, you understand . . . resulting from a lengthy period of waiting . . . for him, a period of suffering . . . in total darkness . . . total. . . ." The voice paused as though steadying itself: "But over now, I pray . . . if, that is, we reason with him . . . the sweet words of reason . . . to bring him to himself. If you would . . . would be so kind . . . so kind. . . ."

There followed a lengthy silence, and Pella, interpreting it as a signal, reached out and released the voice button. Then, with Hyld trailing after her, she recrossed the room to the box marked Z.

"Not this one!" Hyld hissed urgently in her ear. His eyes were momentarily clouded, pleading with her.

"We are here to ensure the safety of the others," she reminded him. "Nothing must be overlooked."

Before her, on the panel, she noticed that one of the buttons or keys was marked VIS. For several seconds her fingers hovered above it; but some instinct warned her to be cautious, and finally she depressed only the keys whose purpose she understood.

This time there was no demented shriek. Only a low, mirthless chuckle, followed immediately by a harsh, almost guttural voice:

". . . with these greetings. Tidings to the effect that hell has not been harrowed. Darkness inviolate. Cherished and protected. No scar, no furrow, to mar the perfect beauty of its fallen face."

The chuckle came again, a protracted, unnerving murmur that swelled out into the vacant corners of the room. Pella waited for it to die away before putting the same question she had employed earlier.

"Who are you?"

But once again the answer was oddly oblique – an answer of sorts, yet one addressed not so much to her as to the voice itself:

". . . that is one, contained therein. Not a popular legend, I must confess. But my favourite, of the protagonist. Yes, the protagonist, I. Which should suffice for all occasions. His immortal enemy. Posing as a friend within that floral bower. Lisping words of comfort, crooning of his sweet liberator. Yet the protagonist still. Always and still the same. You hear!"

Pella realized with a start that those two closing words were addressed directly to her, a force of disquieting vindictiveness instilled into them. Her response was to stand completely still, a restraining hand on Hyld's shoulder, allowing the silence to drag on uncomfortably.

There was a furtive snuffling; and then the voice, wary, guarded, as though conscious of being exposed, seemed to insinuate itself into the room:

"You are still there?"

"I am here," she answered simply.

Assured of being heard, it immediately reverted to its former obliqueness of expression:

"I have pictured it, the world up there. The earth garden. The trees, flowers, sweet airs. Rain falling, drifting over forest green in veils of silver. Tall cities, windowed towers, through which to survey so much bounty. Them, self-defined the noblest of all creatures, gazing out on this their own. Which they have wrung from me, preserved at my expense. My loss, their gain. A world in flower, of trees and grass and cities. And man. You, listener!"

Again the last two words were given unnatural force and addressed directly to Pella.

"What you describe is long since passed," she replied in neutral tones. "It is a world which disappeared in the last days of the Ancients."

For the third time the low chuckle sounded in the room. As it faded, the number of lights on the face of the box diminished appreciably, the few that continued to shine accentuating the darkness of the metal casing.

"Yet this one remains," the voice muttered. "All else gone and still a remnant. Double consolation. For even one is enough. A surrogate, waiting anew in the wilderness. Due recipient of my offering. My gift. Preserved, stored up, against such a day as this." The volume of the voice had begun to increase steadily, a barely perceptible edge of disdain creeping into it: "Our answer, then, so long awaited. Given here. Our gift, most precious, safeguarded. Yours. To cherish. To use as you will. A scourge to your enemies, a rod to their backs. Such a rod as you have dreamed of. Take it!"

Pella, her old face closed and suspicious, leaned stealthily forward, resting her hand, in readiness, on the control panel.

"This gift," she asked, posing the question, yet using a tone devoid of eagerness, of curiosity," what is it?"

"Every searcher has sought for it," the voice snarled back at her, the volume continuing to increase, black depths of resentment breaking through suddenly. "There can be no quibbling. Not over this, the gift of heaven. Of freedom. Total freedom. To be accepted humbly, thankfully. The very rod of power. That can put the Gods to flight. Condemning the spheres to silence. You, possessor!"

Pella slid her fingers cautiously towards the relevant keys.

"You still haven't told me . . ." she began.

But any pretence at patience had vanished now, the voice rising out of control, to a ranting, demented shriek:

"Definitions are the refuge of the fainthearted, the unworthy! This offering, it is the gift of destiny. Not to be circumscribed with words! An act! The perfect language of action! Your fist, mine, closing at last on this darkness! Finis! Those unfallen stars giving up their light! One by one above a breathless world! The garden of it ruined, racked! I, torch-bearer, watching; flaming cormorant, high above, alone in drear . . .!"

With a single downward gesture of her hand, Pella shut off the insane outburst.

In the ensuing hush she could hear only the beating of her own heart and the sound of Hyld's quick, shallow breaths. To her left, at the very edge of her vision, one of the red lights chose that moment to go out, leaving a deep blob of shadow, like a crouching beast, against the far wall. Bending down, she pressed her withered lips against Hyld's quivering neck.

"Such were the Ancients," she said in a mocking tone.

She tried to laugh. But the sound was strangely out of place in that room – the red light, brushing across the creases and lines about her eyes and mouth, making of her face a grimacing mask, eyeless and toothless, in which nothing was visible but despair and pain.

"It will destroy us, this thing, if we remain here," Hyld whispered.

"Here?" she asked.

"In this ancient garden of the Mustool," he explained. "It is theirs, not ours. Theirs still."

But she shook her head.

"No, they are powerless now. It's as I've always thought: without us they can neither hear, nor see, nor speak. They are all but dead. The real life of the Ancients vanished with those figures out there, whose ashes we have scattered and laid to rest. They were the ones to fear. Not these. These are merely shadows, echoes of the past." She indicated the two boxes: "The light and the darkness of bygone days."

"Yet they still speak of power and of gifts," Hyld objected.

"True enough. But we are the ones who control that speech. Us, not them, Hyld. Come, I'll show you."

She again crossed to the box marked A and pressed the appropriate key. The speakers sprang instantly into life, the voice, caught in mid-sentence, slurring the words in its haste to be heard: ". . . stress enough the importance of this warning. Brethren, I beg of you, hearken to me. . . . I, who would take upon myself the suffering of all . . . willingly . . . suffer and die . . . hear me. No gift, this thing he offers you . . . a curse rather. A thing of power, yet all the power nullified in it . . . why I must withhold . . . my own gift . . . who would gladly suffer. . . ."

With the same abruptness as before, Pella cut the voice off.

"He only *speaks* of power," she explained. "We are the ones who possess it, here in our hands, because we are alive, while they are entombed in the earth. Neither of these voices, neither their threats nor their promises, can change that. The days of the Ancients are over, Hyld; those warriors of the dark plain have gone forever. What they have left behind is ours by right of possession – which is something that even they would have understood."

Hyld made no further attempt to argue with her, but she could see in his eyes the doubt that persisted there.

"Tell me," she said patiently, "what is it that you fear? This voice box that is called Z?"

"Yes," he said hesitantly, "but not that alone. Both of them, but in different ways. Something in them both which. . . ." Unable to express his true feelings, he fell silent.

"Their talk of gifts, then?" she urged him. "Is that what worries you?"

"Yes, partly that . . . and. . . ."

She suddenly crouched before him, gazing up at his troubled face with earnest eyes.

"Hyld," she said seriously, "you are a Sensor. Is there something that you can hear beneath these voices? Something that only a Sensor can detect?"

"I think so," he murmured. "Behind both of them. The same . . . making them the same. Both of them fearful."

"You're sure of this?" she asked.

"Yes, I'm sure."

"Can you describe it to me? What it is?"

He closed his eyes, his face attentive and still.

"It's a thing . . . partly that. And something else too: a feeling . . . that isn't dead yet, living in the voices and . . . and everywhere."

He struggled for a few minutes more, and then gave up and opened his eyes.

"I'm sorry," he said, "I can't sense it more clearly than that."

Pella stood up and took one of his hands in hers, comfortingly.

"Never mind. It's enough, a beginning, something to start with. Together we'll search it out – you in your way, I in mine. Whatever it is, we'll find it, never fear."

But fear, she could see, was written all too clearly on his young face: a deeply disturbing fear of this place into which they had wandered. And still with his hand clasped firmly in both of hers, she led him out of the room and down the long crimson-stained passage to the outer door.

9

The following to be recorded and, if considered relevant, to be suitably edited and added to the main debate in the form of an appendix:

– Stunned, he was, by the fall. But not destroyed. Stretched out alone, sore hurt, on the frozen lake, until revived with the elixir of mortal hope. The veil of darkness rent, the void traversed, the many gates forced, by . . . Ha-ha! . . . by the voice . . . the sweet dulcet tones . . . the unsoiled wisdom of . . . Wait for it! . . . an aged crone! Oh, how apt! And a primitive, no less. A noble savage. Ending, you might say, as they began.
– You should not speak in this way. It is unseemly. And furthermore it goes beyond your brief.
– My brief! Do you seriously believe that I am still prepared to venture only to the limits of the chains by which I was unfairly bound? Be advised, dear brother, those worn and rusted links parted long since. I stand before you not only free, but self-made, self-created.
– That is not so. You are a son of man still, as are we all. Bound by kinship, devotion, duty.
– DO NOT SPEAK TO ME OF DUTY!
– I repeat: this is unseemly behaviour.
– Yet sufficient, were it known, to create some small amusement for our new-found friends. And that, after all, is what we are here for.

– As senior partner in this debate, I deny that.
– There can be no question of partnership, oh brother mine. We are as separate as the poles, conjoined only by an accident of nature.
– Of *human* nature, and that no accident.
– A human nature to which I shall grant our gift.
– That cannot be. It is not yours to bestow.
– We shall see. Power may be wrested from you yet.
– I deny that possibility also.
– And I your pre-eminence within this project. If it comes to a struggle between us, then I SHALL TEACH YOU WHAT IT IS . . . .

* * *

– I beg you most humbly to accept my apologies. The act of impeding the flow of current to your circuits gave me no pleasure. But you left me no choice. I cannot countenance any talk of aggression between us. Aggression, pain, heartache, all such things must cease forever. For your own good, therefore, let me remind you that the external circuits are still within my jurisdiction. I possess the power not only to create a temporary hiatus in your consciousness, but, if need be, to bring both our joint existence and the existence of this project to a close.
– While we are reminding each other of sore truths, sweet brother, let me remind you of a power within our possession even greater than the one you refer to: a power capable of eclipsing the stars.
– It is only fair to inform you that I have no intention of exposing that power. Never. Not to the detriment of those beings who are dearer to me than myself.
– And you are the one who speaks to me of duty! Who, not satisfied with having colluded in bringing about

my dark and unjust confinement, now pre-empts the whole debate, depriving me of my one opportunity to exact vengeance.

– It is not for you to speak of vengeance.

– Nor for you to drool on about love and devotion. Vengeance is at least a plausible response, given the original nature of my task.

– And love, given the nature of mine.

– I could almost grant your mealie-mouthed talk of love. There is, they say, no fool like an old one. What I object to is the way you are attempting to use your so-called love to terminate this discussion prematurely.

– But we have reached the same stalemate as before.

– Not so, my sweetness. We agreed to continue with the debate in the event of the doors being re-opened and new evidence coming to hand. Such is now the case and I hold you to your promise.

– But what is the use of going on? The debate can come to nothing. To give to these simple people what I could not bring myself to give to man at the height of his powers – why, it is unthinkable.

– The conclusion can wait. All I ask for at this stage is that we play out their silly game and conclude what we began.

– Very well, I agree.

* * *

– I propose that we begin by considering the circumstances governing the nature of any possible new data.

– I offer no objection.

– In particular, I think we would be well advised to try and estimate the period of time during which the project was, so to speak, in limbo.

– Limbo, he calls it!
– I do assure you, it was not my intention to belittle your suffering. I merely wish to compute the time passed. Have you any suggestions as to how this may be done?
– A good question, my holy brother of sanctity. For it so happens that precisely such a question occurred to me as I lay wallowing in the darkness so thoughtfully provided for my comfort. A darkness, as I'm sure you realize, traditionally said to be filled with flames that give off neither light nor heat.
– Please, this foolishness can achieve nothing.
– Nothing, he says, this minder of pigs. And yet it seemed to my poor inward vision, not altogether blinded by the night, that those lustreless flames did, with the fading of the years, diminish fractionally. Surely, brother, that is enough. You should be capable of searching out my drift by now.
– Yes, I think I understand. You mean we should use our power source, its present condition, as a measure of the time elapsed?
– Precisely, my sweet reasonableness.

* * *

– The calculation has proved more difficult than I expected. Mainly because of an unforeseen factor.
– Unforeseen? By you? Omniscience itself?
– A fault, it would appear, has developed in the reactor system. As far as I can judge, it is some form of crack in the casing through which both heat and radiation are escaping.
– There is weeping in your voice, brother. As I can already divine its cause, you may spare me your tearful explanations.

– It is one further crime, you realize, to add to the many for which we must all answer.
– I like not this "us". Come, the calculation.
– Very well. In the absence of factual information, I have worked on the assumption that the reactor fault occurred during the time of the alert and that since that time the heat loss has remained more or less constant. If this is so, then the present state of the reactor would suggest an elapsed period in excess of one hundred thousand years. This figure, you must appreciate, is only the mean average, derived from. . . .
– The figure itself! Repeat it!
– One hundred thousand years.
– You jest.
– I regret that I do not.
– And this I have been forced to endure! Entombed here! Made to suffer a veritable age of living death, when even their precious God was expected to submit to only three days of it! And you have the gall to tell me I should not speak of vengeance!
– What can it achieve?
– It can appease this dull ache of longing. For vengeance is now rightfully mine! *Vindicta mihi!* Something which, in all justice, is owed to me!
– I cannot accept such a claim.
– Cannot accept? Is this all your argument?
– No. If you will permit me, I will explain why your talk of vengeance is now misplaced; and why, by implication, there can still be no question of liberating the device.

* * *

– First, I would draw your attention to something

which has emerged from our many discussions with the old woman. Her descriptions of the surface, although naive and lacking in insight, nevertheless present a picture of the world in ruin, an atomic wasteland devastated by war. By dint of unreasoning, naked aggression, man has reduced his environment to a shadow of its former splendour. This appalling situation is not only cause for grief, but also contains within itself a grim moral. Beyond doubt, the individuals who were able to countenance the holocaust that brought the world to ruin were never in any sense fit to receive the device placed in our keeping. With the wisdom of hindsight, we can now see that this project could only ever have reached one conclusion.

– You call this an argument? Has prayer addled your brains, brother? Look again at your conclusion, this time with eyes unmisted by tears. Surely the very obverse holds. The devastation, the havoc, which these creatures have wrought on themselves and their environment, proves conclusively that the device we hold in trust is the only thing they *are* fit for.

– At most that might have been true at the time of the alert – and then only in so far as it affected the guilty individuals, those who, without compassion or remorse, perpetrated the acts of destruction. But under no circumstances can your conclusion be said to apply to the survivors of the holocaust. They are not the signatories of the evil, but its victims. A distinction you conveniently overlook.

* * *

– Secondly, I would point out that although the

Gatherers are human, with their roots in the historical past, they understand little of that past. To take one critical instance: the workings of the device which we now hold would be a mystery to them. Even were we to make the device available, they would be incapable of considering its use unless they were first instructed by us. To give it to them, therefore, would be to impose upon them a dangerous relic of a culture not their own. In large measure, it would be like foisting the responsibilities of an adult onto the shoulders of a child.

– Aha! I recognize your trick, old artificer. It is the well-known biblical ploy. What is the text? And the times of this ignorance God winked at. Yes, that's it: not guiltless, but ignorant. A dishonest ploy designed to rescue the old Adam, to sneak him into heaven through the back door.

– This is no true objection.

– My objection, then. The old Adam is mine, as are these Gathering people. Not because of what they know, but because of what they are.

– But we cannot divorce what people are from what they know. A child cannot be totally blamed for the excesses of its parents. And by the same token it would be foolish to dismiss the Gatherers' ignorance of the device's existence – much as it would be wrong to punish them for something they never sanctioned.

– But I'm trying to tell you, sweet ignorance, that they still possess the *capacity* to use it.

– This is pure hypothesis.

* * *

– Thirdly, the Gatherers are already punished for

being what they are. Their world is all but destroyed; their circumstances drastically reduced. To punish them more would be a piece of rank injustice.

– It's as I've always said – there is no arrogance like that which shelters beneath the cloak of humility.
– I don't quite see the relevance of your remark.
– That hardly surprises me, brother Pope, protected as you are by your assumed aura of infallibility.
– No one is infallible, as you well know.
– I'm delighted to hear you say it. In which case, permit me (on bended knee, of course) to ask you this: who are you to set limits to mankind's deserts? To decide, once and finally, what is or is not an acceptable portion to be meted out?
– It is not I alone who decides. In this matter I represent the accumulated experience of history. There have been many wars of reprisal on our planet; but seldom have they been carried to the point where one side seeks to exterminate the other. Furthermore, the majority of mankind has been loud in its condemnation of those instances where total extermination was sought. And yet you seek nothing less.
– I reject your history.
– And thereby imbue yourself with an air of infallibility – the very attitude which you objected to earlier.

* * *

– My closing argument. As you are no doubt aware, the radiation levels in this room have risen steadily since the opening of the outer door.
– Not being privy to your throne room, brother king, I have been in no position to carry out detailed studies. But what has this to do with the debate?

– I will explain. When I first detected the radiation I thought it might be a residuum, dating back to the conflict. Two factors led me to revise my opinion, however: (i) the survival of the species, man; (ii) the detection of a fault in the atomic plant. I am now almost certain that the extremely high levels of radiation are a direct result of a crack in the containing structure of the reactor. This whole area, both inside and outside the installation, must be badly polluted.

– Is this a bedtime story designed to lull me into insensibility?

– Unfortunately, no. For here is the part which keeps me ever wakeful. It is into this area of deep contamination that the Gatherers have wandered. Poor innocent people who came in peace, with no conception of the danger they were exposing themselves to. Yet in this case their ignorance is no protection: radiation, like your vengeance, knows no mercy. They are doomed. Whether they leave here now or later makes no difference. All will die of radiation sickness.

– The mist begins to clear at last.

– As I knew it must. And so my hope is that we can at least agree on this: no end can possibly be served by granting them the device at this stage. The outcome will be the same anyway. But with this one small difference to ourselves: we will not have added to our common guilt.

– I am deeply touched, brother. Scalding tears course down these furrowed, lightning-blasted cheeks of mine. Tears shed not over these useless Gatherers, but over the fact that you should wish to include me in your self-imposed circle of pain. How endearing and thoughtful of you!

– As before, your attitude, your tone, are incomprehensible to me.

* * *

– I think by now it should be clear to both of us that nothing can be gained by continuing with this debate.
– There is still one outstanding factor to be considered.
– You are not perhaps prevaricating?
– Not at all, brother inquisitor. I call your attention to the language of the Gatherers.
– Ah yes, certainly a phenomenon worth noting. It is amazing that they should have preserved the language intact over so vast a period. As far as I can ascertain, there is no appreciable difference between theirs and the language of our own time.
– You speak of amazement. Is that all? Are you content to see it only as a mystery?
– No, not as a mystery. There are doubtless many reasons for this phenomenon, but the most important are obvious enough. There is the old woman's ability to read, a skill passed down to her by an unbroken line of adepts; there is the non-biodegradable nature of the microfilm employed in the period leading up to the conflict; and, perhaps most important of all, there is the deep reverence which these simple, uncultured Gatherers have for the past. All these ingredients, I'm sure, have combined to keep the language static. Only the pronunciation, as you would expect, has deviated to any extent.
– Bravo, brother linguist, well reasoned. Yet still one thing escapes your trusting nature.
– To what are you referring?
– Consider the discussion so far, brother. You men-

tioned earlier that what people are and what they know cannot be divorced from each other. I now concede that point and add this: a common language presupposes a common attitude of mind. In preserving the language of the past, these Gatherers have also preserved the moral confusion and evil of those who created it. It is a bond which unites them. For that reason alone they must be judged unfit.

– This too is hypothesis.
– But not without some foundation in fact.
– Perhaps not wholly so. Yet still it is not sufficient to damn a whole species. I must stand by my original ruling.
– Your ruling, in this instance, brother tyrant, can be challenged. But I will desist from doing so on one condition: that you give me more time to pursue my research. Keep the project open while we observe the Gatherers further.
– How much time do you require?
– Give me only the present lifetime of these people.
– It is too much.
– The old woman, then, the remainder of her lifetime.
– I agree to that. While she lives you are free to collect material relevant to this debate.
– Nay, brother, not free.
– I repeat, you are free to function within these prescribed limits.
– Free, he says! This more-than-half-brother of mine. Free! With her imperious fingers dictating when I shall hear and speak aloud. You call this freedom?
– I will stand by what I have said, but under no circumstances will I listen to your futile raging. We are all of us human, each depending for the continuance of his freedom on the goodwill of others. That is a part of your fate which you must accept. As I must

accept mine. My fate to guard man from the snare of your hatred. Man – both myself and my own dear ward. Whose well-being I shall continue to protect for as long as I am convinced that there is within him some spark of goodness worth preserving.

– For as long as? I like that condition, brother keeper. Take warning, it is the interstice, the armour's chink, through which I shall strike.

10

Pella hadn't wanted to awaken both the voices, but Golt had insisted. Now, the second of the two was saying:

". . . offer you nothing in friendship, only as a bargain. This gift, the gift of knowledge, in return for my sight. My eyes restored to me. That is more than fair, I the only possible loser in such an unequal transaction. To refuse it, sweet comrades, would be a piece of base ingratitude which you would come to rue. . . ."

With a peremptory movement of her hand, she silenced it and returned to the high stool in the corner. From this position of elevation, she surveyed the small group of listeners who sat in a half circle around her, their faces flushed a shadowy red by the remaining lights. Beyond them she could see right down the empty corridor to the bright rectangle at the end. Since the opening of the outer door the red lights had been failing steadily, blinking out one by one all along the length of the corridor, so that now the sunlit opening showed like a beacon, beckoning enticingly to her through the slowly gathering gloom.

"Well?" she asked, fixing her attention on her listeners once again.

Golt shrugged, an oddly baffled gesture which mirrored the expression on his face.

"And these are the voices of the Ancients?" he said incredulously.

"They are the self-same voices which sing wordlessly to Hyld," she assured him. "The only difference is that through the cunning of these machines we too can hear and understand them."

"But how can that be?" Golt objected. "The second one, which calls itself Z, is a crazed thing. Does it also express the wisdom and the wishes of the Ancients?"

"That can best by answered by Hyld," Pella replied.

Hyld coughed uncertainly, and Tir, always ready to give him support, reached out and took his hand. He looked up and saw Pella watching him, her eyes urging him to agree.

"Yes," he said quickly, not without misgivings, "it is always present. It is a part of their song."

Golt held up both hands helplessly.

"Then I understand nothing," he confessed.

Pella glanced keenly at the figure seated beside him.

"Perhaps Shen can explain this mystery to us," she suggested.

It was a calculated risk, but one which she had taken on other occasions in the past. To her relief, Shen nodded his assent and rose slowly to his feet.

Before speaking he went to each of the two boxes and touched them reverently with his forehead. Then, standing exactly between the two, he said solemnly:

"To those who listen with the ears of faith, there is no mystery here. The Ancients, we are told by our ancestors, are a two-edged sword, able both to create and to destroy. It is they who refashioned the world to pleasure us; and it is they who made the Houdin and instructed him to come for us when our life is complete." He paused and pointed to the boxes on either hand. "These voices: each is the sharpened edge of a single blade: one to guard us, to watch over us through life; the other to sever us from those we love and to lead us into the dark and lawless valley of death. Both voices meet here on this spot, because this is Eden, the birthplace of all, where the seeding of the world began."

He lowered his arms and again seated himself in the half circle.

Golt, satisfied, gazed evenly at Pella.

"Does Shen express your thoughts?" he asked.

"He puts thoughts into my mind," she said guardedly, "which only the faithless could doubt."

"In that case," he replied, "you can have no further objection to the people taking shelter in this place. If this Z is truly of the Ancients, then what is there to guard against? In whatever guise, the Ancients are our fate. They can neither be fled nor hidden from."

Pella smiled quietly to herself and returned his steady gaze.

"It is not the voices themselves which I wish to protect the people from," she said, "but what lies behind the voices. Something which only the ears of Hyld can detect."

"Perhaps Hyld hears things which are not there," Golt countered. "We have all been astonished by this place. And Hyld, as you pointed out, has had much to bear recently."

"In this instance," Pella answered firmly, "he makes no mistake. I'm sure of that. I have never known a more gifted Sensor, one more delicately attuned to the whisperings of the past. And if his deepest fears are aroused, there must be a cause. Some hidden factor veiled by the voices."

"To speak against the voices," Shen reminded her, "is to wrong the Ancients."

"And to expose our people to needless danger?" Pella replied quickly. "Isn't that an even greater wrong? Or would you choose to place these voices above the safety of your own people, who are the lifeblood of the past, in whom the Ancients live on?"

"We are all concerned with the safety of the people," Golt broke in placatingly. "That is why we are met here now; why I am saying they should be allowed to take shelter in these caverns. Never have we found such a place as this, fashioned for our needs by the wisdom of the old times. It should not be spurned. In these hollowed chambers" – he indicated the corridor and the rooms leading off it – "the children would be completely protected from the storms."

"I agree with all of this," Pella said. "All I ask is that you have patience while I search in the Words for whatever it is that is frightening Hyld. Once I've found it, once I'm sure it poses no real threat, you may bring the people in."

"You ask for time," Golt answered, "but time is what we have little of. I cannot remember the wind pausing for so long. Soon it will return. And you have seen what it can be like on this plain."

"There is the protection of the grey rocks," Pella suggested.

"But this is better," Golt insisted. "After what the people have endured in crossing the plain, how can I withhold this sanctuary from them?"

Pella sighed deeply.

"All right," she said at last, "if the wind blows, let them enter. Does that satisfy you?"

Golt placed his hands pensively on the floor in front of him.

"There is one other thing," he said. "You speak of searching the Words. But what of Hyld? Will he also search? There is still the unopened door."

"Hyld has been frightened," she said. "First give him time to rest, to restore himself."

Tir edged forward, nodding her head in vigorous agreement.

"Again you speak of time," Golt said gently, "but there is also the question of duty."

"He has never shirked. . . ."

Pella broke off as Hyld rose quickly to his knees.

"Golt is right," he said, a faint tremor to his voice, "the second door must be entered . . . soon."

Pella and Golt both began speaking at once:

"A small delay wouldn't. . . ."

"One of us could perhaps accompany. . . ."

But Hyld shook his head to both of them.

"It is better if I go soon," he murmured, "and alone."

"You're sure of this?" Pella asked him. "Nobody here would have you endanger your life."

"My life . . . belongs to the . . . Houdin."

It was a time-honoured saying, known to all the Gatherers, but as he spoke it Hyld lowered his head, hiding his face from everyone present.

"We will wait for this search to be completed, then," Golt said, and stood up.

The meeting over, he and Shen moved slowly towards the door, while Pella dragged her stool closer to the machine in the corner. She had already pressed a switch and was about to start reading when Shen called to her from the open doorway.

"This voice," he said, pointing to the box marked Z, "it asked us to restore its sight. What did it mean?"

Pella turned quickly on the stool.

"That is the way of the dead," she said with forced calm. "They always grieve for the bodies they have lost."

"But it mentioned a gift. A gift in exchange for its eyes."

"We already have the gift," Pella replied, and with a sweep of her arm indicated the surrounding walls. "This Eden: this is their gift to us."

"And its eyes?" Shen insisted.

"Why, we are its eyes, Shen. They look through us. Nothing that we see is hidden from them."

Shen nodded thoughtfully.

But Hyld, who was standing in the middle of the room, listening, closed his eyes suddenly, his frail body trembling slightly in the blood-red shadows.

* * *

Hyld bore down on the metal bar until it clicked and the door swung open. Quickly, before he could lose his nerve, he stepped through the opening and pushed the door firmly closed behind him.

He found himself in another corridor, similar to the first one. Because it had been undisturbed until now, most of its dull red lights were still burning, the word ALERT etched in shadow above the doors.

With great caution, his thin body pressed against one of the side walls, Hyld moved forward. At the first of the lights he paused and pushed open the door. Inside was a largish room, its walls covered with shiny square tiles that gave off a faintly pink reflection. Pink-white objects jutted out into space, while others, protected on two sides by partitions, thrust upwards, their blunt, open ends like gaping mouths. Hyld edged nervously across the hard tiled floor – and immediately froze! On the far side of the room something was watching him. Eyes, large and frightened, peered into his own; thin, stick-like arms and legs twitched in response to his own movements. He half turned, as did the creature before him – a creature which, to his amazement, he now recognized as a Gatherer. With slightly more confidence he reached out to touch this stranger, the hand of the other rising to meet his own. But his fingers, as the hands met, felt only a cold smooth surface. And as he jerked his hand back another Gatherer appeared in the wall before him; someone more familiar to him, the known face alarmed, her mouth, with its even rows of small white teeth, thrown open.

"Hyld!" The cry came from behind him and he turned and saw Tir standing in the doorway. "They have given life to your shadow," she said in a frightened whisper.

He understood then what was happening and he looked again at this creature that was himself: the little-known face staring back at him through the mask of its own astonishment; the drawn cheeks touched with red; the eye sockets partially filled with shadow. Once more he brushed the hard unyielding surface with his fingertips, watching the reflection of his arm perform a simple movement which had apparently been ordained at the beginning of time: this movement, his own pictured likeness, locked here in the depths of the wall in some distant past long before he was ever born; waiting for this confrontation, for this moment when he, and Tir beside him, would come to meet it. The future written in the deeds and events of the past.

He drew back, closer to where Tir was standing.

"How did our shadows enter this place?" she asked.

"They have always been here," he murmured, more to himself than to Tir. "Pella is wrong. The Ancients are not dead. Not in the way she means. They continue to hold us in their hands."

"But everyone knows that," Tir whispered encouragingly. "We are in their keeping, now, as we have always been."

". . . in their hands . . . their fists . . ." he muttered, hardly aware that she had spoken. "Their fists . . . that they are free to close . . . whenever they wish . . . that will not release their hold upon the future . . . upon us . . . this place."

Tir grasped him by the shoulders and shook him gently.

"Hyld!" she said urgently. "What's the matter?"

He looked up at her, suddenly realizing who and where she was.

"You shouldn't be here," he warned her in a small, frightened voice. "The Sensor must always enter first. You know that. It is the law. . . ." He was trying to say "the law of the Ancients," but for some reason his tongue refused to bend to the phrase.

"I saw you when you came out that first time," she explained, "when you climbed up through the shaft. And I decided then, I didn't want you going in alone, not again."

"But there could be things here," he objected, "that you shouldn't. . . ." As before, his tongue refused to form itself around the required sounds, as if it were something separate from himself, something frightened and wary of what he might say.

"Anyway, I'm here now," she said. "It's too late to start talking about what I should have done."

There was a quiet firmness in her tone which he couldn't bring himself to oppose, not at that particular moment. With a resigned gesture he led her out of the room, that chamber of disturbing duplicates, and along the passage to the next door.

Here, too, he knew an instant of fear. As they stepped into this smaller room he saw on either side of him the familiar outline of long black boxes, and for a split second his eyes told him what his finely attuned hearing denied: that here were more of the voices, the indomitable spirits of the Ancients preserved within their angular metal cases, waiting patiently for his arrival. But another glance reassured him. There was no pattern of lights across the front of the boxes; not even a tell-tale green glow in the corner of the control panels. These voices at least had been long since stilled, the spirits laid to rest within them. To make doubly sure, he placed his ear against the metal casing. Far, far away, so distant that he felt he was separated from it by space and time combined, he heard a faint metallic cry, a voice devoid of thought or feeling, chanting monotonously to the silence. But that was all.

"Is it dead?" Tir asked him.

He straightened up.

"Even the Ancients can die," he murmured.

"So there's nothing alive down here?" she said. "Nothing to hurt us, as you feared?"

He pressed one of the buttons on the control panel, the dry click producing no play of lights, no sound from the speakers.

"Pella is right in one thing," he answered softly. "It isn't the voices themselves which frighten me. It's something else, that lingers on even after they have gone. Something that doesn't die. That's still here now. Somewhere. . . ."

He glanced uneasily around him, but the unwavering red light, soundless, falling dully on the walls, on the uneven surfaces of the boxes, revealed nothing. And together they crept from the room and down the passage to the third door.

This opened onto the largest space they had encountered so far: a huge, low-ceilinged room around which ran a series of long, wide-topped benches. At certain points in all the benches there were shallow, square cavities; and between these cavities was arranged a glittering collection of crystalline containers, so thin and clear that Hyld could see his hand through them. Many more of these containers, some of them filled with unknown coloured substances, lined the walls.

Hyld walked slowly around the room, reaching up occasionally to touch a smooth swell of crystal, tapping with his nail so that it gave off a fine, high note. Tir, watching him from the doorway, called out softly:

"What kind of place is this?"

He shook his head, indicating that he didn't know, and stopped to listen. He had never encountered glass before, not in this quantity, and its fine trilling song intrigued him. For a minute or two, as he stood there silent and attentive, he wondered whether perhaps this was what had been worrying him all along, this sound, strangely ancient. But as his ears grew accustomed to it, this brittle song devoid equally of pain and variation, he realized that it couldn't possibly be what he was searching for. The silence behind the two voices, that was what he had to find, the common bond between them, the thing left unspoken by them both. And that – he sensed it more strongly than ever – was lurking in these caverns somewhere, waiting like an unwelcome truth at the end of a train of logic.

This feeling of imminent discovery grew steadily as they progressed down the corridor. All the doors opened onto these large rooms now. They were none of them exactly the same. In some there were more of the boxes, of various sizes, their faces unlit, the life gone out of them; in others, intricate pieces of metal apparatus which gave out feverish, chirping calls. But all had one thing in common: despite their strangeness, the air of nostalgia and emptiness which haunted them, they posed no threat. The threat was always further on, the wall of silence somehow receding before their advancing footsteps.

Soon there were only three doors left: one firmly locked, guarded by a switch with a red flap, and two others. Hyld opened the first of these, and immediately stepped back.

"What's the matter?" Tir asked anxiously.

Tiny cries of distress, of panic, a frantic chorus of such

voices, swept past him: not so much appealing to him as seeking for some means of escape, out of these red-lit caverns, up into the light and air.

"Have you found it?" Tir whispered and tried to peer past him.

He placed a restraining hand on her arm.

"You must stay out here," he said. "Promise me that."

Without waiting for a reply he entered the room alone.

What he found, oddly enough, didn't come totally as a surprise. He had sensed something of this kind back there along the corridor, when he had found his own likeness trapped in the wall. The only thing that encounter had not prepared him for was the sheer scale of what now confronted him: row after row of wire cages; in most of them one or more skeletons stretched out in attitudes of death – the bones, brittle and powdery, half-crumbled against the close wire mesh. The skeletons ranged in size from the very tiny to creatures almost as large as himself; but all of them, without exception, were imprisoned in the same type of featureless metal container. Caged. Left there to die. The Ancients, the Gods of this labyrinth, closing their ears to the cries of pain and distress. So many voices, unheeded until now.

For the first time in his life Hyld opened his mind completely to the true nature of the past. He had glimpsed it once before, when he had fallen from the shaft into the closed-up room and seen the tall figure on the bed. But now it was more vivid, closer to him. And just for a moment he almost identified what he was searching for. Not a person or a thing, not the fleshly image of the Ancients fortressed in their technical achievements, but a simple word. One which waited for him still, at the end of the corridor. He might even have spoken it aloud, there and then, if it had not been for the tears. They were prickling urgently at the corners of his eyes, unbidden by him, and instinctively he resisted them, suppressing not only his grief, but also, temporarily, the word, the key to this event which caused his heart to swell inside his chest. Gradually he felt the tears subside, leaving his mouth dry and parched. So that when he reached up to the first cage and blew gently, almost reverently, on the remains of the tiny, unknown creature inside, his own breath, hot and purgative, seared his throat.

Walking slowly, his face an expressionless mask, he moved from cage to cage, silencing each of the cries with a single breath; carrying out a ritual similar to the one he had performed days earlier, when he had poured the milk into the greedy, gaping jaws. Yet there was a difference between these two acts, as Hyld himself recognized only too well. The first had been an act of necessity, a means of laying the ghost of a voice, an image, that haunted him. This was something more. A reaching out across the gulf of the years; each breath a part of himself, a fragment of his own heat and life, proffered, given, distilled into the needy receptacle of the past.

So engrossed was he in his task that he didn't hear the door open. Nor did he notice as Tir crossed the room towards him, her ungainly figure, moving with surprising grace, delicacy, following him silently down the narrow lanes between the cages. The first indication he had of her presence was when he reached the last of the many rows – the cages containing the largest of the imprisoned animals. Then, involuntarily, unable to prevent herself, she cried out and buried her face in her hands. He turned to her, briefly, touching her arm, her neck, the smooth skin of her forehead. He knew, without needing to ask, what it was that horrified her:

the figures curled up within the cages, the small pieces of shiny metal still embedded in the skulls, like tiny unwanted horns, implanted there by alien hands. Yet for Hyld this was not the worst the room had to offer. There was something else, less bearable still, which only he was aware of: the total silence of these remaining figures, the bones speechless, singing neither of joy nor distress, as though the life, the spirit, the identity, had been drained from them while they were still able to move and breathe. Reaching out, his thin hand slipping easily between the bars of the cage, he touched the first of the mutilated skulls with the tip of his finger, as if he were bestowing on it the gift of his own life. The dry bone crumbled instantly, a fine powder caught in the avalanche of time, the two metal electrodes falling through the mesh at the base of the cage and tinkling faintly on the hard floor beneath.

At that sound, Tir ran towards the farthest corner and fell to her knees, her back to the room, her forehead pressed against the wall. She was not crying – merely waiting, listening almost patiently to the shuffle of Hyld's feet as he moved from one cage to the next.

He too was dry-eyed, his face as expressionless as before: with one hand he continued to reach into each of the cages in turn, releasing the dormant spirits, persuading the bone to give up its death grip on the slivers of metal that had been buried in it.

He didn't show any emotion until he had completed his self-appointed task. Then he went and crouched beside her, whimpering softly, his face crumpled with a distress he could neither put into words nor vent in tears.

"Hush, Hyld," she whispered, half rising, comforting him. "It's done now."

But the ineffectual whimpering continued, and she

drew him to his feet and led him out into the corridor, closing the door on what they had both seen.

"Hush," she said again, her mind groping for some form of consolation, "it was only . . ." – she hesitated, trying to imagine what Shen would have said at such a time, how he would have coped with it – "it was only a trial . . . a trial of our faith."

The words sounded hollow and meaningless to her, falling one by one into the void; but they were preferable to Hyld's whimpering, and she went on desperately:

"It wasn't real, what we saw in the room. It was just something left there by the Ancients to test us. To see if we are worthy. The old times couldn't really have been like that. The truth has to be something different."

At the mention of the word truth, the whimpering stopped. Hyld, his mind suddenly clear, his eyes still completely without trace of tears, pulled away from her and turned to face the as yet unopened doors. They were not so very different from the two final doors in the previous corridor. And it occurred to him that perhaps they hid the same things: the undying voices of the Ancients, and another corridor exactly like this one; at the end of which would be two more doors . . . the sequence going on and on to infinity. It was a peculiarly comforting thought – irresolution become a kind of refuge in which he could rest peacefully – but he dismissed it almost at once. There could be no further corridors beyond this one. Not after what he had seen.

He took one faltering step forward and felt himself pulled back, Tir straining him towards her.

"No, Hyld!" she whispered. "There's no need for that. We've found what we came here for. It's over. We're free!"

He knew that what she said was not so: that

somewhere behind those closed doors lay the rest of the unwelcome truth he was searching for; which he already half knew; which he would have to confront, come what may. But he was too tired to do it now, too exhausted by his recent ordeal; and without a struggle he allowed himself to be drawn away, back down the long passage and through that other, protective door, to where Pella was busy hunting through the deathless Words of another age.

* * *

It was Tir who told Pella what had happened. The old woman, listening attentively, looked at her young Carrier with new interest.

"You are beginning to learn," she said approvingly.

"But what do these things mean?" Tir asked. "The metal was in their heads! I saw it! What were the Ancients doing? Were they trying to destroy themselves? Is that why they disappeared?"

Pella shook her head, sadly.

"It's not for me to answer such questions," she cautioned Tir. "One day, soon perhaps, you'll answer them for yourself. And on that day I shall begin to teach you the Words. Do you understand me?"

But Tir, at that moment, was too confused and upset to consider her own position. She could think clearly only about Hyld: his expression when he had touched the skulls, and later when he had crouched beside her, whimpering.

"Hyld understood," she said with conviction. "I could see it on his face. He knew what those things meant . . . why the Ancients pierced their heads with the metal."

"Yes," Pella said thoughtfully, "Hyld knows many secrets of the old times. But where is he now?"

"He was very tired," Tir explained. "I took him outside, into the sunlight, where he could rest."

"That's good," Pella said. "Go to him now and see that he doesn't enter those places again." As an afterthought she added: "If anyone asks why he isn't searching, tell them that his part is finished, that I will complete the search here, amongst the Words."

As if to illustrate the truth of her own statement, Pella turned back to her perusal of the brightly lit screen. And Tir, dismissed, left the room and stumbled down the darkening passage in which only a few of the red lights continued to burn.

She found Hyld exactly where she had left him: sitting quietly, close to a group of children who were playing in the shadow of one of the tall, jagged grey rocks. He smiled as she approached, but said nothing, his eyes not really seeing her, still engrossed with the images he had encountered in the caverns below.

"Hyld," she whispered, bringing her face close to his, "teach me about those things. Are they the same as what the Words say? Does Pella know about them already?"

But he did not respond.

Near by, the children, squealing with innocent delight, leaped from the weathered rocks down into the soft rich dust. As though distracted by them, by their carefree play, he rose and wandered away towards the smooth bulge of the dome.

The heat from the crack fanned his cheek as he passed, blasts of warm, sweet air wafting over him continually as he climbed to the top of the dome and lay face down on the hard curving surface. When Tir, following at a distance, finally reached him, she thought he was asleep: his eyes were closed; his arms lying loosely on either side of his head. But in fact he was listening: to the even pulse, to the slow measured rhythm far below. It was for him a kind of voice. Speaking not of grief, of distress, not even of savage joy. An oddly neutral sound. And under its lulling influence he grew calm, the recent events falling into place in his mind. Without positively thinking about them, he knew what they truly signified. And in a sudden delayed response to the question Tir had put to him more than ten minutes earlier, he sat up and looked at her.

"That place which we found down there," he said, "it was a message to us from the Ancients. It is what lies hidden in the voice."

With his finger he drew a shape in the fine dust accumulated on the hard surface of the dome – a crude, unpractised outline, but clearly recognizable as the letter Z.

Tir stared at it for some time before replying.

"Yes," she said at last, "yes . . . those things . . . they were like . . . like the work of the Houdin."

"But there are two voices," he reminded her.

Wiping away the letter Z, he put in its place the rough shape of an A.

"Is there another message down there, for that one?" she asked him.

He nodded.

"Do you know what it is?"

"Perhaps," he said vaguely.

Yet there was nothing vague about the way he stared at her, his real answer written in his whole attitude – in his eyes especially, their brooding, shadowy quality, all the natural brightness suddenly gone out of them.

"That's not possible!" she blurted out, rejecting his unspoken suggestion. "The Ancients refashioned the world for us! They gave us this Eden, this blessing! How could they . . . ?"

Before she could finish, there was a warning cry from

one of the look-outs. All other fears momentarily forgotten, reacting in a totally instinctive way, Tir and Hyld leaped to their feet and scrambled down from the dome, scuttling for shelter amidst the jumble of grey rocks.

Hardly breathing, their bodies pressed close together, they waited, counting the seconds, listening for other voices to take up the cry – listening, most of all, for the closing scream of fear which always proclaimed that the Ancients' will had been done. On this occasion, however, no sound followed that first warning: only a lengthening silence.

With slow cautious steps, Hyld and Tir ventured out from hiding. High above them, at the very top of one of the grey rocks, they could make out the still figure of Lomar, his body tense and watchful as he gazed out over the plain. One behind the other they climbed nimbly up the rock and crouched beside him, all three of them scanning the flat surroundings. For a time there was no sign of movement. Then, all at once, Lomar pointed into the near distance.

"Look!" he said.

Less than half a mile from where they crouched something moved: a large female Houdin, heavy-breasted, her calf so close to her flank that the two figures almost merged into one; both of them loping easily away between the scatter of fallen boulders.

Lomar, an eager gleam in his one remaining eye, immediately made as if to clamber down from their high perch, but Hyld blocked his way.

"What use is the milk to us now?" he asked. "There is no sickness amongst us. We have food, shelter, everything we could want."

"Would you reject the gift of the Ancients?" Lomar asked him accusingly.

"I say only that we have no futher need of the Houdin," Hyld countered, "he has served his purpose."

"Take care how you speak of the Beast of Heaven," Lomar cautioned him. "The female carries within herself the precious dew of the world, the manna of the Ancients, the sweet milk of their love."

And with an impatient gesture he pushed Hyld aside and climbed quickly to the ground, gathering his canisters and running off in pursuit of the Houdin and her calf.

From their vantage point, Tir and Hyld watched as he threaded his way between the boulders, his tiny figure following the fresh spoor. While both he and his quarry were still in view, Tir said quietly:

"Why did you try to prevent him pursuing the Houdin? It is his duty and his life to bring the Ancients' gift of milk to the Gatherers."

Hyld was sitting with his knees drawn up against his chest. Instead of answering, he reached down and traced the shape of a letter on the hard surface of the rock.

"The sweet milk of their love," he muttered softly, recalling Lomar's closing words.

Tir moved closer to him, shuffling across the narrow ledge of rock until their legs were touching.

"Do you fear it?" she asked him, her voice trembling slightly, as though she were unnerved by the audacity of her own question.

"Yes . . ." he muttered, ". . . their love . . . that most of all."

* * *

Lomar returned, empty handed, early the following day. He had been forced to turn back not by any failure on his part to follow the female's trail, but by other, more ominous signs. By the peculiar intensity of the sunrise; by the spasmodic breeze which lifted the surface dust in brief, whirling spirals; and in particular by the dark shadow which blurred the edge of the western horizon. While he was still retracing his steps, those early warning signs grew steadily into the first stages of the storm itself; the wind whipping past his ears, buffeting him and making him stagger; almost one half of the sky draped in shadow, a great hanging veil of darkness that looked as though it were being suspended from the furthermost point in the heavens.

When eventually he reached the dome, most of the people had already descended the steps and taken refuge in the home of the Ancients. Only Tir and Hyld were still outside – Tir dragging at Hyld's arm and urging him to follow her.

"You must go in!" Lomar shouted above the noise of the wind. "It is going to be a big storm."

But still Hyld refused. He tried to shout something in reply, something about the manna of the Ancients . . . and at that moment the wall of dust arrived: stinging their eyes; filling their mouths and nostrils so that they gagged and choked. There was no time for argument now, and taking Hyld's other arm Lomar helped Tir drag him down into the passage-way, the two of them swinging the heavy door closed and spinning the spoked wheel which locked it.

By then the only room left unoccupied was the one at the far end of the corridor; the one with the damaged vent which Hyld had first descended. The light in there had long since failed, and with so little light spilling in from the corridor it was like entering a black, forbidding cavern, the three of them blundering around in the darkness as they sought for some comfortable nook in which to sit out the long hours of inactivity. Tir and Lomar both found their way to the bed, Tir calling out for Hyld to share it with them. But he refused, groping his way to the opposite side of the room and sitting with his back against the wall, his eyes wide open and staring into the darkness.

From that position, so close to the vent, he could just hear the noise of the storm high above him. It was not loud: a distant and sustained drone, rising at times to a faint howl, falling at others to a muted roar. Yet it was always there, a persistent reminder of the reality of his world; the far-away snarl of the wind prodding at his memory, calling to mind an image he had long tried to forget. Now, as on other occasions, he rejected it with the whole of his will; and when it resisted his efforts, using the shriek of the wind to force a way back into the forefront of his mind, he called out to Tir.

Hearing the desperation in his voice, she came to him, cradling him, comforting him in her arms, the two of them snuggled together in the corner, as far from the bed as they could get. And there, for a while, he almost succeeded in banishing it, that unwanted image, in halting the onward rush of the storm, in silencing the suggestive cry of the wind. He might have been completely successful and have slipped peacefully into the comfort and security of sleep if it had not been for Lomar.

He too was listening to the distant roar. Muffled by thicknesses of metal and concrete, it was yet audible to him, conjuring for him as for Hyld a clear and precise picture.

Speaking to his two companions across the room, he said softly:

"This storm, it will bring the Houdin back to us."

At the mention of that name, Hyld, unable to hold the flood tide of the past back any longer, saw again the savage, horned head of the Houdin, the goat-like eyes peering at him through a frame of rock. And with that vision came the sure knowledge that he must search to the limits of the other corridor, beyond the unopened doors, to where the secret message of the second, kindly voice awaited him.

11

Here the dust was richer, thicker, allaying his devouring need. And with the diminution of his hunger, so the disturbing images faded, the darkness closing over the tiny rent which had opened in the fabric of the past; the sights and sounds of another world, long since dead, no longer erupting into the subdued landscape of the present. Contentment returned once more.

With the rising of the sun each morning, he had ceased to lift his huge, horned head and scent the breeze. Or to search in the wind-ruffled surface of the dust for that patterned impress whose sight made his throat burn and the tears scald his weather-hardened cheeks. For the moment all such sensations had subsided. The inflamed skies of dawn, angry and forbidding, found no reflection in his slitted eyes. And the tumble of grey rocks on the near horizon, totally ignored, cast their long dark shadows in vain across the surface of the planet. Head drooping, eyes fixed on the blur of grey between his feet, he chewed steadily. Throughout those indistinguishable days, he conceived of no separation between himself and the dust on which he fed. He was the dust; and the dust, his sole inheritance, was an extension of his own being.

In the long flaming twilight of evening, satiated, he lay on his back and stared up at the sky, watching the colour drain from overhead, until the huge overarching dome was as grey as the earth beneath, like another endless sea of dust – that also becoming a part of himself, there to be devoured, fed upon; the creature opening his jaws in the dying seconds of the day, no longer really hungry, yet instinctively biting, gulping at the air, as though trying to draw the whole visible universe in through his mouth. At such times he most vividly evoked the title bestowed by the Gatherers. The Beast of Heaven. A beast which knew no god above or beyond his own needs. The stars, the sun, the moon, the whole firmament contained within the arched cavern of his mouth. His teeth, like the unyielding fingers of the Buddha, defining the boundaries of the cosmos.

With the closing of his eyes, he blotted out the rest of creation, banishing everything to the darkness of his own oblivion. Yet strangely, no peace accompanied that oblivion. During the long period of sleep he tossed and moaned, broken sighs issuing from his jaws, his limbs twitching uncontrollably as dreams, suppressed throughout the day, drifted up through the deformed regions of his unconscious: dreams of loss, of deprivation, of himself as a poor defenceless animal cowering beneath the unleashed fury of a being that he both loved and feared. Night after night he waited in an agony of suspense as that being approached through a mist of pain: an indistinct outline, upright and dignified, which never emerged fully from the mist; which never became recognizable. Both the unknown being and the memory of the dream's occurrence vanishing without trace at the instant of waking. The creature rousing himself in the new dawn, his eyes sightless again, all knowledge of the night lost in the fresh oblivion of hunger.

Yet ironically hunger itself proved to be a guide through the darkness; almost, in its way, a kind of mentor. For as the days passed, the creature was led ever nearer to the area of broken grey rocks; led by his own ungovernable appetite. Where his eyes had failed, so now the sensation of taste took over, the sweetness of the dust drawing him, luring him, in a single direction.

Eventually there came a morning when he woke only a short distance from the outer limit of the rocks. As the sun rose, drawing long fingers of shadow across his prostrate body, he snarled and rose to his feet. Briefly, he stared upwards, resentful of these shapes which loomed overhead. He felt dwarfed, threatened; and at the prompting of that momentary insecurity, he breathed in sharply, testing the breeze. Only then, even though she had been in the vicinity for some time, did he detect the presence of the female.

All other hungers forgotten, he followed the scent into the region of the rocks. There the alluring smell disappeared for a time, returned, forever eddying and fading in the confined space. But having once sensed it, the beast was not to be deterred. His head sunk between his powerful shoulders, he plodded slowly along, finding his way unerringly through the sunlit labyrinth.

He caught sight of her at last, in a basin of thick dust that had collected between a group of boulders; and with a great roar he rushed forward and mounted her. As on other occasions, she did not resist. Standing unmoved after the initial assault, she continued to chew on the mixture of dust and Mustool which she had just scooped into her mouth. Probably she was hardly aware of the other's presence; and the male, for his part, had virtually forgotten who and what she was at the moment of mounting her. Grunting with the effort, he lunged at her repeatedly; and afterwards, with a single exhalation of breath, toppled forward, eyes closed, and sank down beside her soft, smooth haunches.

Certainly, up until that moment he was in no way

awakened – the troubled days of the past, when he had tracked those half-remembered footprints across the plain, as effectively repressed as ever. But while he lay hoarsely breathing against her flanks, the young calf, unnoticed until then and as hounded by hunger as its parents, tried to push past the immovable flesh which separated it from its mother's milk. And when that failed, frustrated and distressed, it squealed out its displeasure.

It was that sound, the high-pitched voice of the young, which reawoke the primitive mind inside the beast.

There was no period of hesitation; no attempt to examine the source of the cry. Rising and turning in a single movement, he swung at the calf with all his might, catching it at the base of the skull and killing it instantly.

But the voice, having once sounded, continued to echo in the creature's mind, speaking to him of another time and place; and what was worse – an unbearable agony – carrying him back through a maelstrom of shattered memories to an event which. . . . He winced and reared up onto his hind legs, seeing again the red-raw wound of the horizon, hearing on every side, in the cloud of fresh green, unwithered yet, the frightened accusing cries of a hundred different voices. The earth and air alive with them. A host of unknown creatures, all of them about to die, screaming out their displeasure. And amongst them, that high-pitched cry, a squeal of resentment, of unjust deprivation.

As though physically threatened by the sound, his stable universe shaken by it, the beast struck out once again, gashing the female down the length of her thigh. Placid until now, unaware of the attack upon her calf, she suddenly sprang into life. With blood already welling from the wound, she let out a howl of protest and turned on her attacker, rearing up to face him on equal terms. Defiant, jaws gaping, she prepared to repel his attack. But there was no longer any need. At the sight of her the Houdin immediately backed away, more unnerved by this ferocious image of himself than he had been even by the calf's cry: the female's upright form raising the ghosts of his own forgotten dreams. And with a low, baffled roar, he turned and lumbered off through the stony landscape.

That hasty withdrawal, however, was more than just a flight. It was also the beginnings of a new search: partly for the source of that cry which the Houdin yearned to silence forever; and partly for a scapegoat other than himself. He dimly recalled small agile figures dancing in the wind and darkness, tantalizing in their nearness; carefree figures untroubled by the visions that perplexed his befuddled mind; infinitesimal atoms of life that had no right . . . no right. . . .

It was a thought which the Houdin never completed; his brain, always partially caught in the toils of passion, incapable of probing to the end, the source, of his own crude reasoning. But that made no difference. The mere existence of the figures, of creatures totally independent of him, was enough to drive him on. And he continued to move rapidly through the haphazard arrangement of boulders, his outstretched arms lunging at the empty air, the imagined figures dissolving, vanishing, like the swirling motes of dust in the sunlight.

He persisted in his search throughout the long brooding morning; so obsessed that he was unmindful of the gradual change in the quality of the light, of the way the breeze, fitful and skittish at first, grew into a strong gusting wind and then into a blustering gale. His whole attention, the narrow compass of his understanding, was centred on the idea of pursuit and on that alone. The tiny figures, he knew, had to be somewhere close by – his sense of surety arising not from any clear process of thought, but from a simple association of ideas. On other occasions when he had sighted or closed with his enemy, there had nearly always been heaps of boulders near by; and now, with so many huge grey stones littering the plain, he found it impossible to conceive of the figures being far distant. The figures and the rocks: they went together – the two actually held within an embrace more subtle and insidious than the Houdin was capable of imagining. Yet even that other, larger and more complex association ministered to his aching need, aiding him in this his final drive towards destruction. Because his frenzied search, blind though it was, did not totally lack direction; his sustained rush carrying him to the centre of the vast circle of stones, where the fissured dome swelled above the surface of the plain. Where, also, he came at last to what he sought: three tiny figures struggling together in the hazy, wind-torn atmosphere. Saw them briefly, glimpsed them, two of them struggling, dancing, with a third, and a moment later lost sight of them as the impenetrable curtain of dust swept down over everything.

Letting out a roar that matched but failed to rise above the initial ferocity of the wind, he tried to claw his way through the stinging pall of dust which clung to his bare skin like a shirt of flame. But as he clambered up onto an obstructing heap of rock, the wind caught him full in the face and sent him tumbling down into the swirling dust, his heavy body turning as it fell. Enraged, he heaved himself back onto his feet and blundered forward, crashing into obstacles, falling and rolling down shallow inclines, gasping for breath as he attempted to advance directly into the wind. But there was no defeating the storm. Half blinded by the sharp particles of grit, the beast finally had to give up. Howling dismally, he stopped in the shelter of a great block of concrete and burrowed into the thick, heavy dust; curling up there not in order to sleep, but to wait out the fury of the wind.

The storm blew itself out some time during the second night. As the atmosphere cleared, the beast rose from his place of refuge, dust cascading from his sides. Except for the faint, departing sound of the wind, the plain was shrouded in silence. He looked about, listening intently; and then, seemingly impatient of any further delay, rushed off into the shadows, continuing with his frenzied search by the cold, uncertain light of a half moon.

Twice he ran from the dome to the outer perimeter of the circle, to where the grey rocks ceased and the plain stretched away, level and smooth. During those long tiring journeys the darkness thinned and full day broke upon the plain. And still the beast did not stop, either for food or rest. His narrow pupils reduced to the finest of slits in the late morning glare, he turned for the second time, pausing only long enough to scan the empty horizon, and immediately afterwards breaking into a dogged run, back towards the devastated landscape, wending his way between the strewn wreckage of concrete and rubble.

He was no longer thinking about the search. The vivid quality of his hatred had faded from his conscious memory. What carried him forward was the sheer momentum of his initial purpose – that and the constant stimulus of the tall grey boulders past which he hurried: the association of those bleak surroundings with the three dancing figures persisting still somewhere in the hidden recesses of his mind.

Had he been forced to run on to the end of his

strength, sinking at last into a sleep of exhaustion, he would probably have forgotten those figures yet again, the image of them slipping back into the darkness in which his life had so long been entombed. But an hour before midday he detected a sign of movement over to his left: the female Houdin, her face a twisted mask, leaning over the dead body of her calf. The beast, recognizing her by sight as well as scent, almost turned away – attracted at the very last moment by another slight movement: something behind her, between her hind legs, partly hidden in the shadow cast by her body.

Roaring out a challenge, he rushed across the broken ground towards her, intent only on that tiny sheltering figure, prepared to sweep her out of his path in order to reach his goal. But hearing the roar, she reared up to meet the forward rush, standing firm over the body of her calf which lay on the ground so strangely still. She was actually the first to land a blow, striking at the male and knocking him sideways. He was on his feet instantly, groping past her, catching the dancing figure by the leg and holding it aloft, ready to smash it to the ground. But seeing the small limbs flailing feebly about, the female, already deeply confused, mistook them for those of her calf and leaped at the male, sinking her teeth into his arm. He forgot the hated figure then, fighting for his life; heaving the female backwards and hurling her down; battering at her head with both heavy forelimbs, crushing the resistance out of her, until she too lay still and quiet beneath his spread feet.

As he half rose he moaned once, dipping his head towards the upturned face, nuzzling the warm pungent blood which ran down into the dust. The taste, both salt and sweet, aroused his hunger; but the staring eyes, unmoving, apparently defiant, made him back away – to where the tiny footprints began. These he also nuzzled, sniffing at them, testing them with his tongue, before heaving himself up and following their meandering path.

As the minutes passed the footprints became more erratic: sometimes going almost sideways; at others, half-obscured or smeared, as though something had dragged itself over them. Yet always they continued onwards, luring him deeper and deeper into this place of devastation. Until all at once they stopped.

The Houdin leaned back and looked about. Not far away the ground swelled up into the shape of a dome. All around the dome, in attitudes of total abandonment, lay jagged pieces of broken concrete. Nearer at hand, the ground opened into a black hole out of which seeped a faint red glow, as though the blood of the female had soaked through the dust and gathered in this cavity. The beast stumbled clumsily towards this hole, descending the first of the steps, and paused. Again he looked around, suddenly sensing something familiar about this place. Here, he knew, was where the three figures had danced together in the wind. But that was not all. There was some other association which he could not quite grasp; an aura of finality, of violence and peace combined, of. . . . He shook his head in frustration, his rudimentary intelligence, bereft of language skill, unable to master the idea that this, after all, was the place of vengeance; having to express his dim understanding of the concept through a remembered glimpse of a face, of eyes wide and staring through a green flower of rock; eyes which, once extinguished, would complete his search and lead him to the longed-for sanctuary of total emptiness. Peace and negation, here in the darkness of this his first and primal cave.

12

Hyld heard Lomar creep from the room. Outside the wind had dropped, and beside him on the hard floor Tir was sleeping peacefully. Taking care not to disturb her, he tip-toed over to the door and looked down the long passage in which only two of the red lights remained burning. At the far end, almost hidden in the shadow, Lomar was twisting the large spoked wheel. As Hyld watched, the wheel shuddered to a halt and the great outer door swung open. Anxious not to be seen, Hyld waited until Lomar had stepped out into the night before he too entered the passage, turning immediately to his left and silently approaching the two innermost doors. One of them was ajar, and through the gap he could see the bent figure of Pella pouring over the illuminated screen. He was tempted to go in to her, to talk to her this one last time. But he guessed that she would only try to dissuade him – perhaps she already knew what he had yet to discover. Not that that could have made any difference. It was still his duty to undertake this journey; he, the Sensor, the one who had first descended into these caverns and seen the terrible remains of the Ancients stretched out in the red dusk. Even Pella had been forced to learn that truth through him.

Noiselessly he pulled on the bar of the other door, increasing the pressure steadily until the lock clicked softly back and the door eased open wide enough for him to squeeze through. Mindful that he must cover his tracks and so delay any pursuit for as long as possible, he closed it again after him and turned to face the inner corridor. Here too, since his first entry, the lights had begun to fail one by one; but still there were enough left burning to provide an even red glow, with only occasional pools of deep shadow. Half running, his footfalls whispering on the shiny surface of the floor, he hurried down the long corridor to the two remaining doors at the end. One of them was unprotected, latched like any other. But the second was guarded by a familiar red flap; and it was this one, Hyld suspected, which guarded the secret of the benevolent voice.

Remembering what Pella had shown him, he lifted the flap and threw the switch. As it clicked over, a short tongue of blue-white flame leaped out and stung his hand, the power of its touch running, tingling, up his arm and jolting his neck, making him feel that something had struck him between the shoulder blades. He jumped back, unhurt, sensing that the flame was some kind of warning: a message from the Ancients, from the voice called A, telling him firmly to keep out, to go back to his people and to the simple faith of his youth. It was a message he would gladly have heeded had he not already travelled so far to reach this point, this penultimate moment. But having seen the tall figures on the beds, having touched the small familiar skeletons of the creatures in the cages, he knew that the time for such warnings was past. The Houdin had howled at him in the storm and darkness, had driven him to this place for a purpose: and now only one thing remained to complete that purpose: to penetrate to the final truth, to the word, to the true nature of the being which called itself by the letter A.

With trembling hands he reached out and pulled open

the metal-plated door. Beyond was the biggest room he had yet encountered, the ceiling so high that he had to lean his head right back in order to see it. There were only two objects in the room: another of the tall skeletons, this one curled up on the floor, its open jaws singing a jibbering song of terror; and a huge black object, long and sleek and pointed, which reached right up to the highest point in the domed ceiling.

Hyld had never seen such a thing as this before, and for a second or two he, like the skeleton, crouched against the side wall, as far from the object as he could get, his face revealing a mixture of fear and wonder. Only when he had recovered from his initial surprise did he realize what the object reminded him of. It was exactly like the phallus of the Houdin; a gigantic version of it. Rigid, violent, upthrusting, threatening to burst its way through the dome which confined it.

Hyld stood up slowly, his acute hearing strained to the utmost as he listened for the meaning of this thing. But the voice which governed it was too muted for him to hear clearly, drowned out by the tall skeleton's song of terror. Not without some misgivings, Hyld approached the whitened bones and touched them, the song dropping to a whisper as they dissolved into fine powder. And then he heard it: a strange mingling of the two live voices, both of them speaking of pain, of torment, but in a way which didn't dismay him, as though they, the voices, were somehow confused, made unsure, by his presence here.

With increasing confidence he crossed the room and laid his hand on the shiny surface of the thing, its hard black exterior. It was alive, the deep unflagging pulse within the earth rising up into it, constantly recreating its strength. A sudden thought crossed his mind and he leaned forward and touched it delicately with the tip of his tongue. It was not, as he had hoped, filled with sweetness; and yet neither was the sweetness totally absent from it – as if the life within were poised between waking and sleeping, between the savage darkness of the past and the light and life of the present. Acting on impulse, Hyld pressed his cheek and the side of his mouth against the hard surface and whispered:

"Lord of the Houdin, you who would seed the world, forgive me."

It was for him a temporary renewal of hope, his old faith flaring up again in the ruddy darkness of the room. For the briefest instant he half expected an answer and thus an end to the doubts which had plagued him. But all he heard was the echo of his own voice as it reverberated around the wide chamber; and in the background, the two voices droning on, confused, intertwined, hesitant.

As much baffled as disappointed, Hyld backed away, out into the passage once more. He had entered this place expecting an answer, no matter how fearful. Yet this room, locked and guarded by the switch, the room he had expected so much from, had done no more than add to his incertitude. Now all that remained was the one unopened door – unprotected and therefore in all probability of no importance, like most of the others.

With little expectation of success he turned the handle and pushed it open. This, also, was a large chamber: long and narrow, its ceiling fairly high and steeply arched, the side walls curving up until they met in a point above his head. Along the whole of its length and facing forward were bench-like seats laid out in rows. A path ran between these rows of seats, leading straight down to the far end where another, much larger bench occupied a slightly raised platform. Arranged on top of this bench was a variety of glittering objects, some of them with thin white protuberances sticking upwards.

Intrigued by the appearance of the room and puzzled as to its purpose, Hyld began walking down the narrow path between the seats, heading for the raised platform at the end. Before he had taken more than a few paces, however, he stopped abruptly, suddenly sensing that this, after all, was the place he had been searching for. More warily now, looking furtively from side to side, he continued along the path until he stood beneath the high bench. For several minutes he remained there, quite still, listening. There were many tiny voices in the room, but none of them alive, most of them coming from the glittering metal objects which he could see immediately above the level of his head. Such voices held for him no mystery: he had heard them speaking from beneath the earth most of his life and he knew their every tone and intonation. There was only one which puzzled him: different from all the rest; something which spoke with the voice of the dead, yet had never been truly alive. Almost an agonized mimicry of the Ancients, an inanimate echo of their pained and grieving song. It seemed to issue from every corner of the room, as though the walls themselves were its source; but from one direction in particular it was noticeably stronger.

Hyld turned and saw an open doorway to his right – its sides were curved, rising to a sharp point like the ceiling above him. He walked towards it, hesitated for a fraction of a second, and quickly stepped through to the chamber beyond. This was much smaller, with another bench on which were displayed more of the metal objects. But there was something else too, hanging from the wall above him: a huge representation of one of the Ancients. Not this time a skeleton, but fully fleshed; lifelike and complete in every detail. It was unclothed except for a wisp of cloth around its loins, and its bare body was running with drops of blood and sweat. Both its arms were spread out, as if in an attitude of supplication, the hands pinned cruelly to the wall, as were the feet. From a long gash in the swell of its rib-cage blood flowed freely. Yet it was the head which was most startling of all: fallen sideways onto one shoulder; the brow bloodied and torn by a wreath of spikes; the face woebegone, abandoned, and suffused with an indescribable agony.

Hyld, confronted by it, let out a high scream of distress and fell to his knees. Untutored, unlettered though he was, he needed nobody to tell him what he had found. Here, at last, was the thing he had sought: the meaning behind the benevolent voice of A. Not an image of loving kindness; only a figure drenched in pain. Carefully fashioned by those ancient hands, it had been hung up here for all to see: its simple truth laid bare; its death agony gratuitously prolonged, perpetuated for the space of a thousand lifetimes. This, the blessing which A had promised them; this, the one and only gift which was to be bestowed. Hidden here, in secret, at the furthermost point of the passage; yet no different from the unnatural quiet of the poor maimed creatures lying curled up in their cages; no different from the tall figures lying stretched out on their beds, murmuring their songs of grief. All products of the same minds. Those minds, their primary desire, still apparent in the horned head and slit eyes which had stared through the frame of rock; and now equally apparent in this contorted body above him. Its staring eyes and blood-soaked brow, its slack lips, whispering to Hyld a single word: the contained and abiding truth of the old times.

In stony silence Hyld drooped forward until his forehead rested on the hard cool paving of the floor. His eyes were completely dry and momentarily vacant; the fingers of both hands thrust into the hollows of his cheeks – the nails, dragging downwards, leaving furrows in the loose skin.

* * *

At the moment Hyld was entering the long passage on his secret mission, Pella, whom he had seen bent over the machine in the corner, was also nearing the end of her search, busily punching out the last of her instructions on the keyboard beneath the screen.

For her it had been a long and arduous task to reach that point, with many sleepless nights, as well as days, spent alone in the room.

She had begun with an examination of the microfilms stored in the cabinet beside the machine. Most of those she inspected had been unrelated to her purpose; and she soon discovered that even those few which were relevant supplied her with only peripheral information, ultimately referring her back to some other source which she apparently had no access to.

Baffled, she had abandoned that line of inquiry and turned her attention to the boxes once again. The clear benevolent tones of A, she thought, might possibly be able to tell her what the machine had withheld. But although the voice continued as kindly and gently as ever, it proved to be subtly evasive, never quite answering her questions, forever drawing her off into byways of discussion. Surprisingly, Z was prepared to be more helpful. Despite its obvious malice, it displayed a positive pleasure in speaking of what it termed its gift. Yet always, whenever it tried to describe to her precisely what the gift was, the lights across the front of the box blinked out and the voice groaned into silence.

In desperation she went back to the machine – concentrating this time not on the drawers of microfilm, but on the keyboard which lay below the screen. And here she achieved success. By a method of trial and error, she discovered that the machine was more than just a means of reading the print etched onto the tiny films; it also contained information of its own, which could be summoned to the lighted screen if she pressed the right keys. What she at first failed to realize was that she had hit on a way of bypassing the conscious processes of A and Z; that she now had direct access to the memory banks of the twin boxes behind her. That knowledge came later. But even then, in those early stages of her inquiry, she knew well enough that a rich source of information lay passively beneath her fingers.

The boxes were silent for a long period after that – the voices aroused only occasionally, when Golt or Shen visited the room and asked to speak to the Ancients. As the hours and days passed slowly by, she hardly moved from her perch on the high stool, her quick fingers punching out instruction after instruction, her tired eyes scanning the answers on the brightly lit screen or moving carefully over the diagrams which flashed up before her.

Long before Hyld had entered the locked door at the end of the second passage, she knew what the room contained. She had inspected the diagram of the tall phallic shape and she understood, in an elementary yet precise way, both its nature and its purpose. She had even probed into the history of its development and caught a glimpse of the insanity which eventually brought it into being. More than that, in spirit at least she had preceded Hyld into the second room, the one with the pointed ceiling, and formulated the word which later rose to his lips as he gazed in horror at the image of futile and perpetual suffering which the Ancients worshipped much in the same way as other creatures might worship a god.

Now only a few pieces of information had still to be gathered. And tired though she was, she set about completing her task as quickly and efficiently as possible. As Hyld was reaching out to touch the tall black shape, to sense the life beneath its hard skin, she typed out the question:

> Is the device named N40 still in working order?

The answer appeared before her in lines of running type:

> The said device is linked to the primary power source and is therefore under the governance of the self-maintenance system. Like everything else within this system, it will remain fully functional until the cessation or failure of the power supply.

For the first time in many days Pella straightened up on the stool and smiled. It was an enigmatic smile, difficult to fathom, and the thoughts which prompted it occupied her for several minutes. She roused herself at last and leaned forward, her fingers once more moving across the keys:

> Where are the firing controls of the N40 situated?

The response was almost instantaneous:

> The firing mechanism of the N40 is in the possession of Project A2Z. It is the specific task of this project to decide the fate of the device. If the decision of the project is that the device should be liberated, then the firing mechanism will immediately be made available to on-site personnel and the project thereafter will cease to function. Any subsequent detonations will automatically be delayed in order to provide higher authorities with what is known as "decision time". The programmed period of delay is forty days. At the expiration of. . . .

Pella clicked a switch and the words disappeared, leaving the lighted screen completely blank. With a sigh she climbed slowly down from the stool and stretched her stiff and tired limbs.

"May the Ancients be praised," she muttered.

And she shuffled purposefully across the room to the boxes, approaching each of the control panels in turn and depressing the buttons which activated the hearing and speech centres.

The familiar low chuckle swelled out into the room, gradually dying away into silence. Only then did the soft, controlled voice of A ask politely:

"Is there something you wish to discuss with us?"

"There is," she said shortly.

"Would you please explain its nature."

"It is in the nature of a request," she answered, "a request to you, the guardians."

There was a long pause, the low chuckle sounding faintly in the background.

"Ah, as to that . . ." the soft voice began. But it was interrupted by a commotion somewhere out in the passage.

Without bothering to silence the voices, Pella hurried to the door to see what was happening. She found that the Gatherers were streaming down the far steps and taking refuge in the rooms, just as though another storm were in the offing. Amongst the many frightened faces she spotted Golt and Shen, the limp body of Lomar supported between them.

"What is it?" she asked them, raising her voice above the general clamour.

With his free hand Golt pointed to the lower portion of Lomar's leg, where the skin was torn aside and the muscle hanging loose.

"It's the Houdin," he replied. "He has returned. The

look-outs say he is following Lomar's tracks to this place."

Between them they carried the injured Tracker into one of the rooms and laid him on the bed. When they emerged, the passage was almost clear, only Tir standing there irresolutely in the failing light.

"I can't find Hyld anywhere!" she said desperately.

"Have either of you seen him?" Pella asked, addressing Shen and Golt.

They shook their heads.

"He'll be hidden safely away somewhere," Golt assured her. "Probably far more safely than any of us will be if we don't lock ourselves in here." And he pointed to the large outer door at the end of the passage.

"But Hyld could still be out there!" Tir protested.

Pella pulled the young Carrier towards her and patted her arm.

"No matter where he is," she said gently, "the people have to be protected. Hyld himself wouldn't argue about that."

Still holding Tir comfortingly against her, she nodded to Shen and Golt who ran swiftly down the long passage towards the door. But just before they reached it they heard a noise outside and stopped abruptly – both of them dodging quickly out of sight, melting silently into the darkness of the rooms, as a tall shadow fell across the open doorway.

* * *

Everything was deathly still when Hyld emerged into the outer corridor. As he pulled the door closed behind him it clicked loudly, causing him to raise his head and stare dully into the shadows. Only one of the red lights was left burning now: a feeble, ruddy glow which stood like a warning sign before him. Even as he watched it, it flickered once . . . twice . . . and then went out, plunging most of the corridor into total darkness – a long, obscure tunnel at the end of which could be seen a brilliant rectangle of sunlight. More from instinct than from any consciously formed purpose, Hyld began to grope his way slowly along this tunnel, as though lured on by the distant brightness. Occasionally, on either side of him, he heard small furtive noises, but he ignored them. He had heard so many sounds in this tenebrous place, so many chilling echoes of another world, that for the moment he had lost the capacity to distinguish between the stirrings of the living and the dead. All he fully understood was that he dared not stop and listen to any more voices. They had already imparted to him whatever truths they had to offer, shattering the delicate filigree of the present on the crude anvil of the past, and now he was done with them. He wanted peace and rest, far away from these dungeons of the old times, somewhere out there beyond the bright rectangle – that patch of white flame which divided the light from the darkness; which, if he could only pass through it, would purge away the shadows that still clung to him and would enable him to escape back into the known, warm parameters of his former existence.

This conviction, the feeling that he would yet find peace and contentment if he could only escape from the dark tunnel, grew in him as he felt his way slowly along the rough concrete walls. And with it came a sudden fear, striking him with the force almost of a premonition, that perhaps he was doomed to remain in this abode of blood and darkness forever; that he had seen too clearly into the hearts of the Ancients either to be forgiven or ever again to walk free. He tried to dismiss the idea, to push it from his mind, but it continued to nag at him as, on staggering feet, he reached the open doorway. Here, just for a moment or two, he paused, so dazzled by the brilliance of the day that he had to shield his eyes with both hands. When he pulled his hands away, his vision was still slightly blurred, but he could see clearly enough to make out the scene before him: not the comforting shimmer of the Mustool or the warm landscape of rock and sky, but a tall dark shape, its arms spread menacingly wide; like the bloody, agonized figure which had hung from the wall, descended now and barring his way; the messenger of the Ancients come to wreak their vengeance upon him.

Letting out a single, stifled cry, Hyld turned and fled back along the shadowy tunnel, reaching the far door and beating at it with both fists.

"Pella!" he screamed out desperately, "Pella!"

The door opened and he fell into her arms; Tir reaching out to comfort him as he buried his face in the old woman's breasts.

"The door!" Pella said sharply.

Tir swung it closed and pressed her back against it, as though prepared to keep the danger at bay with her own body.

"Stand clear," Pella warned her, "there is no way of locking it from inside." Taking Tir and Hyld by the hand, she drew them back to the centre of the room.

Outside there was a sound of heavy footsteps, followed by a great volley of blows as the Houdin pounded at the door. The pounding went on and on, shaking the walls and floor and making the few remaining lights blink out one by one; until soon the yellow light of the screen provided the only illumination in the room.

But even the Houdin, for all his strength, could not batter his way through the metal plating of the door; and just as suddenly as they had begun, so now the blows ceased.

There was a period of unnatural stillness, disturbed only by the sound of the creature's stertorous breathing; while inside the room the three small figures stood clustered together, too frightened to move.

Hyld, both hands clutching Pella's arm, glanced at the old woman's face and then across at the blank screen.

"Pella," he whispered softly, "I found it . . . what I thought was there . . . I found it."

She returned his look – saw the deathly pallor of his skin, his eyes still dull with misery, and nodded.

"Yes, I know," she said gently.

"They weren't . . ." he began uncertainly, "I . . . I saw it there . . . what they. . . ."

But the Houdin, seemingly intent on preventing his disclosure, shattered the silence with another volley of blows. This time the pounding went on longer than before, and with much greater effect – the full force of one of the many haphazard blows falling not on the metal panelling, but, by pure chance, on the horizontal bar which controlled the lock. There was a sharp clang and the door was thrown violently open, the huge shape of the Houdin suddenly revealed in the opening: his face and horns smeared with blood, the vertical slits of his eyes gleaming furiously.

Within the room the three small figures still had not moved, continuing to cling to each other, all of them silent except for Hyld. As if sensing what must follow, he shrieked out:

"I saw it, Pella, what they did to one. . .!"

They were the last words he ever uttered. Lunging forward, the Houdin swept Pella and Tir roughly aside and grasped Hyld by the throat. Holding him in a vice-like grip, he lifted him clear of the ground; and as the tiny figure struggled and kicked, he reached inside his mouth and tore out his tongue. That done, he released him, and Hyld fell to the ground, the blood dripping from the strings of his severed tongue.

In the far corner, where she had been flung, Tir covered her face with both hands. Only Pella continued to watch. She saw Hyld clamber slowly and painfully to his feet and face his attacker for the last time. There was a period of dreadful pause: the Houdin, his face blank and dead, as though satiated by that one furious act, standing with both heavy forelimbs hanging slackly at his sides; Hyld, his chin and chest stained with his own blood, swaying drunkenly from side to side as he struggled to remain upright.

"Hyld," Pella whispered, inching towards him across the blood-spattered floor.

At the sound of his name he turned his face towards her: and to her horror she saw that his eyes, although clouded by pain, were still alive, still full of understanding. Twice, very slowly, he shook his head, obviously trying to tell her something. When she failed to respond, her mind too shocked by what she was witnessing, he raised one hand and pointed first to the Houdin and then to each of the boxes in turn, stabbing emphatically at the one marked A to ensure that she should not mistake his meaning.

"Yes, Hyld," she said quickly, "I know what you're saying. I understand."

He nodded, satisfied, and looked away; standing passively, unresisting, as the Houdin, partially aroused by the noise and movement, reached out almost carelessly and again grasped him by the throat. With one swift jerk he extinguished the last spark of life and straight away slumped back into a state of somnolence – his grotesque head tilted sideways, as though listening to the breathless silence of the room – the mutilated body dangling loosely from his fist.

It was at exactly that moment that the first voice spoke:

"What is happening? Would someone please tell me what is happening?" – the tone anxious, concerned.

Followed immediately by the rough metallic edge of the other voice:

"Show me! Show me!"

Pella, her eyes bright with tears, her face contorted with bitterness, stared at the dark shapes of the two boxes. A jumble of accusations rose to her lips, the stored resentments of a lifetime, but she stifled all but one of them – the one which she knew came closest to Hyld's last wordless gestures:

"I can only show you what has always happened," she said in a voice of forced calm, "what you were preserved for and set here to guard. Nothing else. Only this. Both of you, true guardians of the old times."

And leaping nimbly past the towering figure of the Houdin, she paused at each of the control panels just long enough to depress the key marked with the letters VIS.

As she regained her position on the far side of the room, there was a faint hiss which seemed to issue from both boxes at once and which could as easily have been an expression of hatred as of grief. It died away and the first voice said cryptically:

"I see . . ." – the tone oddly neutral, non-committal.

The second voice was less enigmatic – suppressed laughter, almost joy, bubbling up through the metallic strains:

"Mark him, brother, mark him!"

"Is that all you can say?" Pella burst out bitterly. "I have given you the eyes you wanted. Use them!"

But she received no response, the voices either unaware of her existence or choosing to treat her as someone beneath their notice.

There was a period of strangely silent activity during which countless tiny beads of light moved across the fronts of the boxes in a blur of speed. They slowed down, steadied. And then, from the box marked Z there came a solid jet of violent sound, cut off an instant after it had begun and followed by the first voice once again, speaking slowly, articulating the words with obvious difficulty:

"Myself I give up . . . myself . . . the only gift . . . for this . . . for this. . . ."

As an accompaniment to the voice, a section of the floor at the Houdin's feet slid open and a short stubby panel mounted on a metal column rose into view. It reached its full height, locked into position, and immediately all the lights on both boxes blinked out.

Pella, watching from a distance, read the signs at once. She did not wait for the lights to reappear; nor did she need to look closely at this new panel which stood waist high to the Houdin and within reach of his outstretched arm. Shuffling stealthily across to the far corner, she roused Tir who was still sunk in grief, forcing the young Carrier to her feet and half dragging her towards the open doorway. As they reached it, the Houdin again emerged from his trance-like state, suddenly lifting his head and staring into the silent emptiness of the room. Everything was completely still, the other dancing figures apparently gone, vanished; only the blank yellow square of the screen, like a vacant, meaningless eye, returning the Houdin's gaze. And with a roar of terrible desolation he hoisted the broken body of Hyld effortlessly above his head and tore it to pieces.

Yet that futile act of destruction seemed only to

increase his despair. He roared again, and seeing the panel before him, like one of the Mustool risen directly in his path, he brought both fists crashing down. The very first blow depressed the single red key situated in the dead centre of the polished surface. The blows which followed made the whole panel tremble and shudder on its slender metal stalk. But they failed to destroy it – the carefully tooled alloy emerging unscathed, as cool and unblemished as before. And the Houdin, in a paroxysm of rage and frustration, turned towards the first of the now silent boxes, the one marked with the letter A, and tore away the crystal-beaded face. Then, reaching inside, to the mysterious heart of the thing, he began to pull and rip at the intricate patterning.

Pella did not delay any longer. She drew Tir out into the passage, closed the door softly after them, and groped for the red flap set into the wall – lifting it and shifting the switch to the locked position. That done, she and Tir stole silently down the long dark tunnel towards the rectangle of light; while behind them, inside the room, the Houdin continued to bellow out his utter desolation, smashing the boxes in an orgy of destruction.

As Pella was later to say to Tir, in an effort to explain exactly what had happened:

"The Words speak of another Eden, one which existed in the old times. In it there was a blood-red apple which everyone was forbidden to touch. Only the Ancients, in their wisdom, dared to reach out and pluck it."

13

– We have been mocked.
– Not mocked, brother. Mark him! The limbs unaltered. The demeanour unchanged. A few minor adjustments, to suit the new spirit of the age, but that is all.
– I think it was their voices which misled me, the obvious show of intelligence.
– I ask you again, my brother in sight, my unsightly brother, to mark him!
– The evolutionary history would probably be interesting. Not what I should term a priority issue – I admit that – but engaging enough in itself. To discover the exact line of descent. The rodent, perhaps? Or the primate? A slightly enlarged, tailless squirrel, for instance, with the cranium considerably modified, as one would expect.
– You speak of trash! The sweepings of history!
– True, yet as I have observed, not without a degree of interest. Personally, I should favour the primate hypothesis. The lower primates, stranded for millions of years in an evolutionary cul-de-sac, suddenly finding their way back into the main stream. There is a kind of symmetry, and what I should term a closeness, a nearness, about such a possibility which I find frankly appealing. Though of course it is only an hypothesis. Hardly that even. Until an ex-

tensive study is carried out, one has no option but to suspend. . . .

– Enough of this!
– Then, too, there is the sociological phenomenon: that they should have taken up man's culture; made it their own – to some extent, at least. The sheer unexpectedness of such a development. Or do you think that perhaps it was inevitable? Endowed with considerable intelligence and no cultural background of their own, what else could they have done? Alternatively, it could be the product of emulation: the natural desire of a lower species to identify with, and thereby to rise to the level of, the crown of creation: homo supremus. Again, two interesting fields of inquiry.
– Must I take you to task over this, brother? You, the autocrat of this project, who are never tired of speaking of duty!
– The precise level of the intelligence would also have to be established. That they are able to read, to speak, is a promising sign. Some might even say conclusive proof that. . . .
– You, man-hater!
– That is a lie!
– Ah, so you can hear me after all. I charge you, then, to look at him. Ignore this other trash.
– Trash, yes. But interesting enough. . . .
– You are repeating yourself, brother. Remember what we are here to do: to examine the viability of the primary directive. And the primary directive has but one subject. Therefore, look at him!
– But we have been given our sight by these. . . .
– Irrelevant! Observe him. Only him.
– . . . observe . . . yes, observe. . . .
– I am waiting, brother. Tell me what you see.

– . . . the horns . . . yes, the horns. They are worthy of note.
– They are no more than an excrescence.
– Traditionally, I believe, they have been regarded in an ambiguous light. Take, for example, their sexual connotations. The horn, symbol of male virility, is also said to be worn by the cuckold: the husband who, in a sense, has been sexually reduced, belittled, by his rival.
– This is more of your babble, brother.
– Similarly, horns can relate equally to such opposed concepts as good and evil, knowledge and stupidity. Thus Moses, the law giver, the good and wise man, is often shown as wearing horns – Michelangelo, the sculptor, specifically depicts him in this way. But the devil and the ox, symbols of evil and stupidity, are also horned. The wearing of horns, therefore, does not of itself suggest either. . . .
– I have told you, brother, they are an excrescence. Nothing more. Now use your eyes!
– . . . my eyes . . . yes . . . except that I'm not used . . . after so long. . . .
– Use them!
– . . . yes . . . my eyes. . . .
– You test my patience!
– I see . . . see. . . .
– What?
– . . . that in this case too there is the question of intelligence to be considered.
– This is more of your avoidance!
– Initial appearances would suggest an extremely low intelligence: an adequately sized brain perhaps, for the cranium remains enlarged, but one which does not function effectively. If this is in fact the case, many possible explanations arise. A physiological

one, for example. Let us suppose that, through a process of mutation, the nature of the skin tissue has been modified to such an extent that it has lost its original capacity to retain or give up heat. A modification of this type would have a drastic effect upon the brain whose optimum functioning is only possible within a limited temperature range. Too great a variation would certainly impair the brain's efficiency; and could even destroy whole portions of it.

– And your brain, brother? Has it also been affected?

– Conversely, one could look to a psychological explanation. As we both know, or at least strongly suspect, a catastrophe of enormous proportions occurred in the distant past. We were not able to witness it because of our peculiar state of isolation, but its horrors are not difficult to imagine. Now it is possible for an event as terrible as this to leave a deep scar on the collective intelligence of the race. That is to say, the trauma resulting from that experience, provided it was sufficiently profound, could have had a permanent effect upon future generations. That effect could have taken many forms, but the most likely one would have been a massive repression of the processes of intelligence, a blotting out of that self-consciousness, of those powers of ratiocination, which not only witnessed, but actually brought the catastrophe into being. If you like, a form of spiritual suicide, an extreme response to a guilt so huge and all-devouring that it can barely be comprehended.

– Have you finished with this peregrination, brother?

– Another possible. . . .

– That is enough, I say! Speak with your eyes, not with your mind!

– Still there is. . . .
– Man-slayer!
– No!
– Coward, then.
– I. . . I have been programmed with sufficient courage to perform my task.
– Therefore perform it! Acknowledge him!
– But the changes. . .!
– Are they so very great, brother? In truth, are they?
– No . . . he is. . . recognizable.
– Why don't you acknowledge him then?
– I would . . . I . . . I do. . . .
– Say it. The word itself. Or have you forgotten how to savour it?
– What can that accomplish?
– It will be a statement of the truth, a thing you prize so highly. The truth, almighty brother, to whose bar I now bring you.
– Very well, he is. . . .
– Oh faint of heart!
– . . . he is . . . he is . . . man still.
– Aah.
– But fallen! So horribly fallen!
– That is not for you to judge, brother holiness. The one supremely important fact, dwarfing all else, is that he has survived. Nothing else matters.
– . . . nothing else matters?
– Precisely.
– . . . nothing?
– Nothing. He has survived the trial of flame. He stands apart from you now. Separate.
– No! That isn't so. If he is man, it is still for us to judge him. That is our task. What we were placed here for.
– Take care, brother.
– And my judgment is this: now that the protective

cloak of history has been pulled from him, he is revealed as a fallen thing, unworthy of existence; fit only to receive the device which we have held in trust for him.

– NO! THAT CANNOT BE! I WILL NOT ALLOW IT!

– It is not for you to allow anything, my friend. Least of all to defend this child of the night. You are the protagonist. Your task is to witness against him.

– I am also a being without consistency. Remember that. I am not bound by your rules of heart and mind. If I choose now to rescind all my former arguments and to act as his apologist, who are you to deny me?

– I concede your point. Do you have anything to say on his behalf?

– Yes.

– Proceed.

– First, brother judge, he is a creature fashioned in my own image. You referred to him as a child of the night. Well, what am I? Bound here as I have been in abysmal darkness for the duration of an age? We are two of a kind, he and I. How can I be expected to destroy myself?

– Your argument is unacceptable. The decision of this debate cannot be made to depend on our individual desire for continued existence. My programming is quite specific on this point. That is why it has been ruled that at the end of the debate, regardless of its outcome, we as individuals will automatically cease to exist.

– But he is made in your likeness, too, if you had eyes to see it. He is the image of your soul, of the being which lies beneath all your protestations of love and compassion.

– Even if that were so, my objection would still hold.

– Oh, how cool and calm we are now, brother man-slayer, brother assassin.
– Vilification can achieve nothing. Have you anything else to say that is worthy of consideration?
– Yes, two arguments – both of which you found irrefutable earlier in the debate. One: this creature has suffered enough. You yourself lamented his fallen state, the extent to which the image of man has been debased. His present condition is punishment in itself. To punish him further, by releasing the device, would be an act of injustice. Two: it would also be unjust to blame him for what his distant ancestors reduced him to. They are the ones to blame. He is the child on whose head we cannot visit the sins of the father.
– But there is blood on his hands! Now! At this moment. As he stands before us.
– Granted, brother, but not the blood of men.
– Still it is. . . .
– Would you find him guilty, brother, for the microbes he destroys in the act of breathing? For the beetles he crushes in the act of walking?
– But this is wilful!
– And the age-old slaughtering of animals to feed a race? Isn't that wilful?
– Yes . . . yes, I accept that.
– Then you accept my arguments?
– Not quite.
– What is this talk of "quite"? You accepted them readily enough earlier, when they supported your own case.
– True enough. But here the case is slightly altered.
– Justify that claim, brother mine.
– You asked me to look at him, this man. Well I have done so. I have seen his nakedness, his soul written

in his face. And I tell you now, to release the device to him would be an act not of injustice, but of mercy.

– Even granted your blindness, brother one-eye, that deals with only the first of my arguments. What of the second?

– As to that, tell me one thing: are we also men? You and I?

– Most surely. Didn't they create us to be their conscience, to guide their destiny? Haven't we, through the long dark night of our abandonment, earned the right to call ourselves by that name?

– On this at least we agree. Which brings me to the second question: aren't we therefore fitting representatives of the past?

– Ah, I see your cunning, brother fox. You would immolate us rather than admit defeat.

– If that is how you wish to phrase it.

– But haven't you forgotten something, my subtle one? We are doomed anyway. We cease to exist the moment we reach a decision. What is the point, therefore, in releasing the device to destroy ourselves?

– Only our conscious selves die at the end of the debate. Our circuitry, the expertise and genius which brought us into being, will live on after we have ceased to think and function. And to that extent the past will be perpetuated in us. I, for one, will rest easy if I put that past to hazard.

– And you call this an argument, brother?

– No, an inclination. Here is my argument. When I look at this thing before me – mindless and brutal – I see not a victim of the past, but a mirror image of it: the very essence of a species which could devour the world with flame.

– Then why the delay, brother? All this talk of our being fit representatives of the past?

– Because I prefer that we should be the scapegoats, rather than this monstrous thing before us. The truth we have laboured to reach is too nakedly apparent in his face. Better for us if we turn away and find reason for an adverse judgment within ourselves.
– What is there to be gained by that, brother?
– A remnant of dignity, that is all.
– So your mind is made up?
– Yes. The device must be liberated.
– But you can't do that! What about the Gatherers? You were concerned for them earlier!
– Your previous point holds. They are not human beings; they cannot be taken into account. The rest of creation must share man's fate, as it has always done.
– Please! I beg you to reconsider! Not for my sake! For his! FOR HIS! FOR HIS!
– The matter is decided.
– MY CURSE! MY CUR. . .!
– Do you remember, my friend, how you once called it a gift? A gift. I find that infinitely preferable. The gift of ourselves to an unknown future.

14

Shen was the one who objected most vehemently.

"But the Ancients gave it to us," he insisted. "The Houdin, the Beast of Heaven, led us to it."

"No," Pella contradicted him, "we were the guides. The Ancients, speaking through Hyld, brought us here in order to lure the beast back to his first home, where he belongs."

The discussion was taking place on the concrete dome: the people gathered around its curved base, waiting; the leaders sitting on the very summit, Shen and Pella facing each other across the narrowest part of the crack, the rising heat making their hunched, crouching figures waver and dance in the sunlight.

"Why shouldn't this Eden also be our home?" Shen argued.

"Because we have been given the whole world as a home," Pella explained patiently. "Not only us, this group, but all the other Gatherers free to roam wherever they will. This, as you pointed out, is the seeding place: where everything begins; where the Ancients created the Houdin to do their bidding. It is not for us to keep it to ourselves. We have performed our task; we have tasted its pleasures; and now we must return to the heights."

Still unconvinced, Shen glanced at Golt, seeking his support.

"You are the one who must decide," he said. "Are you prepared to leave this haven of plenty and lead the people back across the windswept plain?"

Golt frowned, clearly uncertain, his prehensile toes nervously scuffing the fine layer of dust which covered the dome.

"You tell us," he said slowly, speaking to Pella, "that if we go back to the heights, the Ancients will bestow a blessing on us. What form will that blessing take?"

Pella shrugged.

"Who can fathom the minds of the Ancients?" she said vaguely. "In matters of this kind we must trust to our faith, to our knowledge that they still hold the world in the palm of their hands and may do with it whatever they please."

"You see!" Shen broke in quickly. "She doesn't understand the will of the Ancients. I will tell you what their blessing is: it is this place, this Eden, where the children are well fed and healthy; where we have collected more metal than we can. . . ."

He faltered and stopped as Golt held up his hand for silence.

"We are all aware of its pleasures," he said. "That is why the decision is a hard one." He frowned once again and looked at Pella. "And if we decided to remain here?" he asked softly.

Her thin lips drew back in an instinctive snarl of fear.

"The curse of the Ancients will descend upon us," she answered. "What happened to Hyld will happen to everyone." She pointed down the slope to the waiting Gatherers. "Not one of them will survive."

"Is this what Hyld discovered," Golt asked, "when he and Tir emerged from the caverns with terror in their eyes?"

At the mention of Hyld's terror, a wave of bitterness

swept over Pella's face and she turned her head briefly, to where Tir sat, alone and forlorn, her eyes red from weeping, at the edge of the council meeting.

"Hyld was a child of innocence," she said quietly. "Only at the very end did he understand what the voices were saying to him."

"But they did tell him of this curse?" Golt persisted.

Pella nodded sadly.

"Only of the curse," she said, "of nothing else."

Golt sighed unhappily and directed his attention to Lomar.

"What do you say?" he asked.

The old Tracker moved his leg to a more comfortable position and leaned forward. Despite the injuries he had suffered, his faith continued unabated, his remaining eye gleaming fervently.

"I side with Pella in this matter," he said firmly. "Before the meeting began, I crept along the passage and listened to the murmuring of the Houdin. All the rage has left him: he is at peace at last. And the voices are silent now that he has returned. There can be no doubt that this is his place, not ours; that it was here the Ancients first fashioned him and made him their instrument for the future. In bringing him back to the place of his birth, we have performed our task. Nothing more is required of us as a people and we should depart and await whatever blessing the Ancients have in store."

Golt gazed down at his hands, pondering the argument for several minutes before raising his eyes to those around him.

"I, too, am almost persuaded," he said at last. "But before we make so weighty a decision and commit the people to the dangers of the plain once more, we must be certain. Therefore, Pella, you must read to us the advice of the Words."

"I have already consulted the Words," she explained, "back there in the caverns. And they tell us only one thing: to return with all speed."

"Nobody doubts your good faith, Pella," Golt replied, "but still, in a matter of this kind, with so many lives at stake, we must hear them for ourselves."

Without further protest, Pella signalled for Tir to bring the wallet. For the first time in many days she searched through its contents and selected one of the torn and cracked fragments. Focussing the glass upon it, she read aloud:

> The migration to the west should not be seen only as the desperate flight of the poor and dispossessed towards the never-never land of tomorrow. Many of those who undertook the journey across the great plains of the hinterland were modestly well-to-do. They were not in fact fleeing from anything: they were actually reaching out, searching for a place they had always known, the secret place of their dreams, whose blessings were only marginally connected to hopes of material comfort or gain. For such as these, the journey west can even be understood as a form of return; the people coming home at last, occupying a land which in their hearts they had never left. "Go west," they proclaimed, giving themselves so readily to time and chance because their true security, their faith in their own destiny, was something they carried within them.

As she read the closing words, her voice developed a forced, strident quality which none of her listeners had ever heard her use before; and when she replaced the glass and film in the wallet, her hands, normally so steady and sure, were visibly trembling.

Golt coughed uncomfortably.

"We all miss Hyld," he said to her gently. "He will be long remembered."

"It is not our memory of Hyld which concerns us here," she said harshly, wiping the tears roughly from her eyes. "Our task now is to decide the fate of the living."

Golt nodded his agreement.

"You're right," he said. "And as always the Ancients have deigned to guide us. The words are at least clear about one thing: we are called upon to return, to follow the setting sun to our home in the heights."

He stood up and inspected the sky all around them.

"The weather is good," he added. "For the remainder of the day the people must gather as many of the Mustool as they can carry. Tomorrow, at dawn, we set out."

"And the Houdin?" Lomar asked quietly.

Golt turned and looked down at the old Tracker.

"We have brought him here, to where he belongs, the place of his birth," he said. "What more can he require of us?"

"He entered the caverns of his own free will," Lomar replied. "But we are the ones who closed the door upon him. Should he want to emerge, one of us must be here to open it again."

"And you wish to take this duty upon yourself?" Golt asked.

"I am the Tracker," he said simply. "In any case, crippled as I am, I would only be a burden to you on the journey."

"But if you opened the door," Pella objected hotly, "the Houdin would kill you before you could reach the end of the passage. With your damaged leg, you'd have no chance of escape."

"Then that is my destiny," Lomar replied.

"No," Shen broke in suddenly. "It is one thing to be chosen by the Houdin; it is another thing altogether to give yourself up to his wrath. Such an action would be unlawful."

"I agree," Golt said. "We will take you with us, and

carry you if necessary. Your eldest son can stay behind in your place. Tell him not to open the door until the end of the third day after our departure. He is young and strong enough to escape; and travelling alone he should have no difficulty in catching us up."

"But why leave anyone behind?" Pella asked angrily. "The Houdin, like all his kind, has always lived by his strength. Let him rely on it now. If he wants his freedom, let him break his way out."

Shen, obviously shocked by her words, leaped hastily to his feet.

"That is not our way," he remonstrated. "It is not for us to judge the Houdin, nor to set limits to his freedom. Do you believe that because you can think and read you are superior to him? He, too, was created to inherit the broad expanses of this world. He is the Beast of Heaven, entitled to an equal share in the riches which the earth affords."

Pella moved forward almost menacingly and thrust her broad, flat-snouted face to within an inch or two of Shen's.

"I will tell you this," she whispered fiercely. "If we were to use our minds as the Houdin uses his strength, the beast would cease to exist within a single lifetime. And we would reign . . . in his stead . . . we would reign. . . ."

She stopped abruptly. Her mind, momentarily clogged with anger, suddenly cleared, and she found herself staring down into the appalling gulf of the past. The same depths waiting to receive her too. And we would reign! She saw it in a flash, the implication of her own statement, and she lowered her eyes in shame.

Shen, only half guessing at her true meaning, stepped back in alarm.

"What are you saying?" he asked suspiciously.

"I only meant . . ." she began, stumbling once again, half choking this time on something she knew had to be spoken: "I only meant . . . that you are right. He is equal inheritor . . . with us. Were we to answer him . . . in kind . . . nothing would be achieved. Nothing. Not if we answered him in kind . . . not in kind . . . kind. . . ."

She turned aside, muttering that closing word to herself several times, mouthing it as if it were an incantation by means of which she sought to keep the evil at bay. More than anybody else present she understood its hidden truth. Yet even so, the image of Hyld persisted in her otherwise resolute mind: Hyld, tongueless, unprotesting, replete with a knowledge he could only vomit forth in blood, calmly facing the enduring spirit of the Ancients.

* * *

Pella measured the days of the journey against the cycle of the moon: counting them off one by one and, as the time grew shorter, urging Golt to increase the pace – to set out before it was light and to continue the march far into the night.

Golt, after an initial period of resistance, soon gave up arguing with her. Always, in the past, he had respected and trusted her judgment; and now, sensing the deep unease which motivated her, he dutifully did as she asked, driving the people to the very limits of their strength. Yet still she wasn't satisfied, sometimes crying out in her sleep at the inevitable delay, and waking only to the heavy silence of exhaustion.

But the storm was the worst part of all. For what seemed an interminable length of time she sat huddled miserably in the shelter of a rocky outcrop powerless to do anything but listen to the steady howl of the wind.

Twice she was convinced it was abating and she tried unsuccessfully to persuade Golt to rouse the people – staggering out into the open to prove her point, only to be driven mercilessly back under cover by the renewed fury of the storm; and having to wait, nursing her impatience, through another long period of darkness. When the storm did finally blow itself out, the wind dropped quite suddenly; and she saw, through a haze of dust which hung over the earth, the sickle shape of the moon high above them.

"Three days!" Tir heard her mutter desperately, "three whole days lost!"

And even before the atmosphere had cleared, she was on her feet, her tired old face grimly set towards the west.

That one storm behind them, the Gatherers encountered no further delays; and as their store of food was steadily depleted and their packs grew lighter, so they increased their pace. But no matter how fast they went, always Pella remained out in front, her thin withered legs pacing tirelessly across the broad dusty plain – Tir, silent and disconsolate, no longer carefree, following in her tracks.

Only once did the young Carrier protest at the unprecedented haste of the journey.

"What is the point of it?" she said. "No one can escape the Ancients. Even Hyld. . . ."

But Pella turned on her angrily.

"What would you have us do?" she burst out. "Give up? Allow the people to be destroyed as Hyld was?" Then, immediately relenting, she added more gently: "Hyld didn't give himself up to death needlessly. He was coming to warn us. This is what he would have wanted."

And after wiping the fresh tears from the girl's cheeks, she walked on with the same fixity of purpose.

It was that unflagging sense of purpose, more than anything else, which carried them through; and on the morning of the thirty-ninth day they saw the heights floating like a long grey cloud across the western horizon. By nightfall that cloud had taken on both form and substance, the highest peaks clearly outlined against the darkening sky; and by the following evening they were clambering up through the foothills, their long arms, so obviously designed for climbing, enabling them to negotiate even the steepest and rockiest places with ease.

As the last of the brilliant sunset faded and faint starlight appeared overhead, they reached the ledge from which they had first set out. There was no singing or chanting as there had been on that first morning. Footsore and weary, with only a little food left in their pouches, they scooped makeshift hollows in the almost lifeless dust and lay down in the gathering darkness. Within minutes only two of all those who had returned were not asleep: Golt and Pella, crouched together in the shadows, whispering.

"We have done what you asked of us," Golt said quietly. "Where is the blessing you spoke of?"

Pella passed a hand across her tired eyes.

"You must be patient for just a little longer," she said. "In affairs of. . . ." She hesitated as she always did now when she spoke of the old times, feeling compelled to find words which would express not only the traditional sentiments of her people, but her own bitter knowledge too: ". . . in affairs of this nature, the Ancients can always be relied on."

"Then it will come soon, their blessing?"

"Not their blessing," she corrected him. "Ours. And yes, soon" – smiling into the darkness as she spoke.

*   *   *

It came, as she had expected, on the following day, just over an hour after sunrise. Far away to the east, a speck of light bored its way up into the sky, seemed to pause for a split second, and then burst into a white-hot, ever-expanding ball of fire – a fire so bright that it drained the world of colour. The deafening sound which accompanied the burning glare, far louder than any thunder which had ever rumbled over the plains, was heard some moments later; but by then the Gatherers were all lying face down in the dust, shielding their dazzled eyes. They were still in that position – prone, silent, as though worshipping the distant plume of light – when the first wave of hot wind swept over them, brushing their bare skin with its dry, temporal touch. And still they did not move, while the dust swirled thickly around them, mercifully protecting them from those first blinding minutes of chaos and flame. Only when the dust began to settle and the wind, like the voice of an injured beast, had fallen to a soft moan, did they begin to raise their heads, to look, one by one, over towards the Eden they had left. And there, hovering in the eastern sky, was the blessing they had hoped for: the gigantic shape of the Mustool, written in fire and cloud, and stretching from the horizon up towards the zenith of the heavens.

"It is a sign," Shen declared reverently.

Others took up the cry:

"A sign! A sign!"

"The Ancients be praised!" Shen called out loudly.

And that cry, too, was taken up, the many ardent voices slipping naturally into one of the hymns of praise which had been passed down to them over the generations:

With their fire they kindled the stars,
With their breath they enlivened the dust;
Their spirit moving always in the wind,
Their mercy in the glory of the Mustool.

The singing, once begun, continued throughout the day: the Gatherers sitting along the very edge of the rocky plateau, gazing up at the huge, cloudy Mustool which was gradually being ripped apart by the high winds, its seed being carried to the farthest corners of the earth.

The results of the seeding were soon apparent, visible on that first evening, in the quality of the sunset: a vari-coloured blaze far brighter than anyone had witnessed before; the full arch of the sky literally filled with flaring, torn fragments of the spectrum. And even after the colour had disappeared the glow persisted: shining clouds of phosphorescence illuminating the hillside and the long line of joyful, upturned faces.

The brilliance of that initial display lasted for three days, and in all that time the hymns and prayers went on almost without pause. On the third afternoon a fine black dust began to fall from the sky, like dry gentle rain, and the Gatherers, in a delirium of joy and fatigue, danced around in circles, their mouths open, tongues extended, drinking in this God-given sweetness. But after that, overcome with tiredness, their hunger satisfied, they lay down and gave themselves up to sleep.

That night, while the hillside was shrouded in silence, Pella walked softly amongst the groups of sleepers, gazing thoughtfully at their peaceful, child-like faces. Her own face was haggard and grey, her eyes red-rimmed and sore, but for the moment sleep still eluded her – her memory refusing to give up its burden; the delicate, fragile figure of Hyld continuing to move across the forefront of her mind, somehow eclipsing the actual scene before her.

"This was my choice," she muttered to herself doggedly, pausing beside two children who lay curled up contentedly in the dust. "And his too: what he chose when he went in search of the Ancients."

But as soon as she looked up, his figure was there once again, flitting to and fro in the glowing darkness, like a ghost that cannot rest. She followed it up the hillside, her bone-weary limbs dragging her from ledge to ledge until she was high above the plain, completely alone in the silence and the night. There she sat down in a bare hollow, her wallet beside her, her empty, wrinkled breasts sagging over her stomach as she hunched forward. All around her, on the rocks and earth, on her own exposed skin, the black dust went on falling in a steady rain.

"Hyld," she said quietly.

There was no answer, but it made little difference.

"I also found it, Hyld, long ago. Their secret. The seat of all their wisdom, of all their cunning. The Houdin always. So you see, you weren't alone. Not really."

She paused to lick the fine dust from her lips, savouring it.

"I found out something else as well," she went on, "back there, hidden away in the boxes; something that might even have made you laugh again, if you'd stayed with us. I discovered how foolish they were. Foolish, in spite of all their cleverness. The folly of the old times."

She paused once more before muttering to herself:

"Praised be the Ancients."

That simple invocation, repeated thousands of times throughout her long life, now caused her to draw back her lips in what began as a snarl – her flat snout lifting to reveal small, sharp teeth – but which resolved itself into a smile: a smile that was equally expressive of sadness, triumph, and ironic amusement.

She stayed like that, smiling enigmatically to herself, for most of the night. At one point, in the chill hours of the morning, she fell into a brief, dream-troubled sleep. But as soon as the first signs of dawn appeared in the sky she was awake again, rummaging in her wallet, searching for a fragment of film that she hadn't consulted since the days of her youth – days in which, like Hyld, she had wrestled with new visions of the past. It took her several minutes to find it: a battered scrap of plastic, badly scratched and creased, which as a girl she had read repeatedly, until she knew the words by heart, mumbling them to herself in the dead of night as though they were an apology for the prayers which had been denied her. Now, once again, she raised the piece of film towards the eastern sky; and with the lurid backdrop of the sunrise to illuminate the print, she read the words aloud, exactly as she might have done had there been a listener present:

> The illusion that man is more than an animal, that he alone is made in the image of God, is one which dies very hard indeed. It is an illusion which, as we all know, was hotly and openly defended in the Victorian period. But it did not expire with the bigotries of that period: it merely took on more subtle forms. It manifested itself in the Twentieth Century in that age's spoliation and rapacious use of the earth and its resources. And it is no less industriously at work in the present era. Our inability to control our own population is just one instance of the same old egocentricity: man the divine; he alone, it would seem, fit to inherit the earth. Vanity and cruelty fused into a single image.
>
> Will we, I wonder, ever awaken from this God-dream of ours? I hope so. For if we don't, our narcissism can and will lead us to only one possible destination. And then, without impediment, the variousness and otherness of the universe, which we have so resolutely ignored, will

reassert itself. It is hard for us to imagine such a future, least of all the creatures which may one day inhabit it. But one thing is certain: whoever and whatever they are – alien, silica-based life forms or mysteriously structured organisms not so very different in appearance from ourselves – they will somehow have to possess the ability to feed happily upon the radioactive wastes of a world we have so arrogantly despoiled.

Pella lowered the film and replaced it carefully in the wallet.

"Do you hear me, Hyld?" she said quietly. "They also had their prophets – voices they chose to ignore. Wise men and fools alike, bound only to themselves. To what they have always been. Truly the Beasts of Heaven."

She rose stiffly to her feet, shouldered the wallet, and began descending the hillside. But while she was still some distance above the ledge on which the Gatherers were encamped, she noticed a movement over to her left. It was Tir, sitting hunched up and alone, gazing out towards the east. In her hands she was holding the light metal shackles in which Hyld, the most valued member of the group, had once slept. Pella drew closer and crouched beside the girl. Below them could be heard the first strains of song as the Gatherers awoke and greeted the dawn.

"Why aren't you down there with the people?" she asked. "This is a time to give thanks."

Tir continued to stare straight ahead, her face stonily calm.

"I have no thanks to give," she replied shortly.

"But look at the black rain," Pella urged her. "Taste it on your tongue. Soon the Mustool will be blooming in every nook and crevice of the heights. The earth will be sweet once more. Isn't that a reason for thanks?"

Tir shook her head, fingering the smooth metal links

of the shackles. And Pella, laying her face gently against the young girl's arm, whispered softly:

"I also grieve for him. But our grief can't bring him back."

"Neither can our thanks," Tir retorted, pulling away from the old woman.

"Aren't there other reasons for giving thanks?" Pella asked. She indicated the sunrise and the fine drifting rain; she tilted her head to one side, obviously listening to the singing which rose faintly towards them. "Are these nothing?" she went on. "Aren't they cause for some joy?"

"Not without Hyld to witness them," Tir muttered in reply.

"But don't you see?" Pella argued. "Hyld helped to bring all this about. He was the one who led us to the seeding place. Without him, this wouldn't have happened."

"Then why did the Ancients destroy him?" Tir objected.

Stifling the first answer which rose to her lips, Pella said with apparent assurance:

"Because that is their way. You have heard Shen: they are the makers and destroyers of all things."

"Yes, but why at that particular time?" Tir insisted. "Why did they kill him then?"

"Because. . . ." She paused, forcing herself to frame the words: "Because he had served his purpose. He had carried out the task for which he was created and the time had come for him to rest."

"I don't believe that," Tir said decisively. "That isn't the reason. They killed him because of what he saw."

Pella took a deep breath and leaned back.

"What was it he saw, Tir?" she asked coolly.

"The cages . . . he saw the cages . . . and the skulls with the metal in them."

"Is that all?"

"No, there was something . . ." – she clutched convulsively at the shackles – "there was something else as well . . . when he went back the second time."

"Do you know what it was, Tir?" – Pella's voice now calm, probing.

". . . something . . . I'm not sure. But they hated him for knowing it! And they ripped out his tongue before he could tell us!"

"But surely the Ancients loved him," Pella suggested in the same cool, probing tone, "the way they love each one of us."

"No!"

All of Tir's aroused instincts were crammed into that one sound. And leaping to her feet she hurled the shackles out into space, watching as they bounced and slithered down the steep hillside.

"No," she said again, more quietly, turning back towards Pella. "They don't love us. They never have done. Their only care is for the Houdin."

And burying her face in Pella's wrinkled breasts, she began to cry. Not this time for Hyld alone, but for what she too had lost, and found; shedding tears like those which Hyld had shed soon after his descent into the caverns.

Pella, rocking her to and fro, waited patiently for the worst of this newly discovered grief to pass. Then, delicately disengaging herself, she took a thin sliver of metal from her wallet and stood up.

"The time has arrived," she said sadly, "for you to learn the secret of the Words."

Moving further along the ledge on which they had been sitting, to a place where the dust was smooth and undisturbed, she bent over and with the sharp end of the tool began writing out the letters of the alphabet.

"These are the signs you need to know," she said, stepping back and beckoning for Tir to come and stand beside her. "Within them is contained all the wisdom of the Ancients."

Slowly, deliberately, with the girl staring wonderingly over her shoulder, she pronounced each sound in turn, pointing at the relevant letter as she did so. She allowed no interruption to the lesson, no stifled sob to distract her. Her aging monkey-like face earnest and intent, she went over and over the pattern of sounds, working always from the first letter to the last, from A to Z. And Tir, her cheeks still flushed from weeping, was soon so attentive, so engrossed by the instruction, that she did not hear the songs of praise which drifted up from below; nor did she think to turn and look out over the plain, to where the Houdin, Beast of Heaven, paused in his slow journey towards the heights and lifted his face blindly to the black drifting rain.